I0554010

Every Month Original
Novels, Stories, and Articles

USA Today Bestselling Writer
Dean Wesley Smith

TABLE OF CONTENTS

SHORT STORIES

FULL NOVEL

SERIAL STORIES

NONFICTION

POEMS

SMITH'S MONTHLY ISSUE #8

Introduction
New Life

A SHORT STORY used to have a very short lifespan. That always bothered me about short stories in the old world of publishing. I would sell a short story to a magazine or an anthology, make a few hundred dollars, and the story would be on the shelf for a week and vanish.

Poof.

No one ever had a chance to see it again. The paper version of the story would go in my file and the electronic file, if there was one, would get dated and become impossible to open.

About one story in a hundred would have some luck and get picked up for reprint anthologies, but that was it. The few hundred (or few thousand) people who saw the story in the short time it appeared were the story's only audience, and they soon forgot it.

Then along comes this new world of publishing.

I spent last year writing new stories and getting some of my older stories out into stand-alone form. I not only published them in electronic, but in paper. Some of the books were only 30 pages long, but each one had only the short story in it.

I loved that. I have over eighty of those books on my shelf.

I felt the stories deserved their own covers and a new life. Not just a spot on a table of contents of a molding old magazine.

So when I started *Smith's Monthly Magazine* eight months ago now, I did a cover for each story in the magazine with the intent of putting the stories out as stand-alone books later. And I will be doing that for the stories in the first issues, starting shortly.

But in the meantime, I started thinking about all the stories that were lost in my files, and about different ways of getting those stories to see print, not only in this magazine, but in stand-alone form.

Thanks for the Support

Dean Wesley Smith

I had four short stories I had published in various places in what (at the time) was called my "Captain Brian Saber" stories. And I had started a novel, but it had gone nowhere.

So as I was thinking about how to bring stories forward and give them new life, it dawned on me that those four Captain Brian Saber short stories, with some fixing and merging and transition material, would be a great start to a novel.

So I started working over the stories and making the four of them meld together. Then I went from where they left off and created the novel that is in this volume, *Life of a Dream.*

The stories are still out there in their original form, but in the novel they take on a new life in a very altered state.

Then, with that success under my belt, I tried to figure out a way to get old files that my computer would not open to open. With the help of some readers on my blog and Google, I figured out how to get to many of those old stories.

One of those stories is called "The Mouth That Walked" in this issue.

It was first published in *Amazing Stories* in 1989. So no one under the age of forty would have had a chance to read that story, and only a few thousand read it in 1989, since *Amazing Stories* at that point was a dying magazine.

So as an extra bonus story in this issue, I'm going to bring the "Mouth That Walked" to 2014. A twenty-five year time travel jump, which sort of fits the subject of the novel in this issue as well.

Life of a Dream is about second chances and being young again.

As the months go by, I'm going to give some of my older stories second chances at times in this magazine. And then they will go on to be their own book for readers to find.

Some of my stories from twenty or thirty years ago deserve a new life. Not all of them, but some.

I hope you enjoy the five stories in this volume, one from *Fiction River: Hex in the City* that is still very much in print, one getting a new life from a 1989 issue of *Amazing Stories* that is long out of print, and the other three seeing life for the first time right here.

And I hope you enjoy the novel with the theme of new starts that gives four other short stories a new life in novel form.

Enjoy.

Dean Wesley Smith
April 8, 2014,
Lincoln City, Oregon

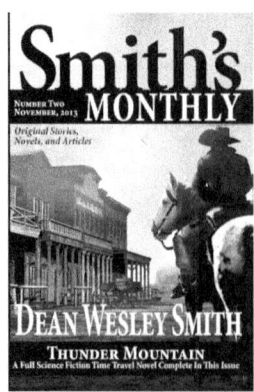

Coming Next Issue in Smith's Monthly
A New, Galaxy-Spanning Novel
in the Seeder's Universe.

USA *Today* Bestselling Writer

DEAN WESLEY SMITH

A PINCH OF HOW ROSIE LIVED

USA Today bestselling writer, Dean Wesley Smith, dives back into one of his favorite topics with this touching tale of being trapped and finding out how to escape.

Rosie lived to bake in her own kitchen, even when he old body wouldn't allow her to do so. But Dot wasn't living for anything.

She learned that from Rosie.

A heart-warming story of the dreams in all of us.

A Pinch of How Rosie Lived

One

THEY SAY THAT when you get old, you lose your sense of smell. For me, I sometimes wish that had been the case. But I suppose if it had, I would have never met Rosie.

Actually, the day my son dumped me into the Shady View Rest Home was the day I most wished someone would have plugged up my old nose. The odor of disinfectant seemed to cling to everything, as if that was the rule of the place and nothing could come in unless it smelled like it came out of a blue bottle.

But there were other smells. The old nurse who tried to smile as she filled out my forms, but didn't really care, smelled of garlic and hand lotion.

The young orderly who wheeled me, with my son walking along beside me, down the wide hall toward my new room smelled of sweat and dried vomit.

And my new room smelled what I imagined death smelled like. I didn't have to be told that the person who had the bed before me had died. It was the way of these places.

Someone would move in the day after I died, too.

But for the moment I sat in the little room and just hated the smell, almost more than I hated my son for forcing me into this place.

"I've got to be going, mom," he said, a fake smile on his face.

But I knew the skinny little bastard I had to call a son didn't have anywhere important to go. He didn't want to be here any more than I did. He wanted to be home with that new wife, sitting in his favorite chair, watching his favorite programs, pretending he had done his duty as a son.

I also wanted to be home, in the house I had lived in for almost fifty years. But I'd gotten sick a few months back, a bad case of my stomach fighting with the lower part of my body. And by the time I was out of the hospital, my son had exercised his power of attorney and sold my house. Then, thinking I was going to die at any minute, arranged that I move into this rest home for my final few days.

Well dying wasn't in my immediate plans. He said, after I stopped yelling at him, that it would be easier and better for me to go ahead and stay at Shady Hills Home.

Easier for him was more like it. This way he didn't have to bother with his old mother. Bother with me was the last thing he wanted to do. And at the moment it was the last thing I wanted him to do. He'd bothered with me right out of my home and I was never going to forgive him for that.

"I'll be fine," I said, letting him hear what he wanted to hear because it would be the easiest and quickest way to get rid of him. "You go along now, and let me get settled."

The little shit patted my hand and said "I'll talk to you soon." Then he almost ran from the room.

Even the young orderly who had wheeled me down the hall gave me a puzzled, eyebrow-up look.

I waved my hand and climbed out of the wheelchair, moving over to check out the television on the nightstand. "Don't mind him," I said. "Some parents dump their children. Some children dump their parents. I just wasn't smart enough to do it first, when I had the chance."

The orderly laughed. "I hear you there, lady. You want me to come back and get you for dinner?"

I turned and stared at the nice young man who stood, half smiling, still holding onto the back of the wheelchair. He had stringy black hair that hung down next to his right eye, a nice, friendly smile, and some light in his eyes. I knew right off I'd enjoy being around him.

"No, thanks," I said. "I can still put some miles on these old legs. Just point me in the right direction and tell me the time."

He glanced at his watch. "Dinner starts at five, in about two hours. Just go to the right down the hall and when you see the big double doors on the left, you're there."

"Service, or do I have to cook my own."

This time he really laughed and his laugh lightened my mood a little. "Full service. But no candles or wine."

"So I don't have to make a reservation, huh?"

"Already got yours in," he said. He turned and headed out the door. "Call me if you need anything. Your bags are in the closet."

"Thanks," I managed to say before he disappeared to the right down the hall.

I moved over and sat down on the bed and glanced around the tiny little room, with its hospital bed, dresser, nightstand, television, and single chair. "So this is where I get to die. Just wonderful."

Two

THE NEW SMELL overwhelmed me in the hall just inside the back door. Dinner had turned out to be overcooked green beans, mashed potatoes, and something that appeared to be chicken, but tasted more like the potatoes. With the express purpose of walking off the food I had managed to choke down, I decided to explore.

The Home, as one blonde nurse's aide so lovingly called it, was a large rectangle. Each side of the rectangle was called a wing. Two nurse's stations anchored opposite corners of the rectangle so that no square foot of the home's halls would be left unobserved from at least two directions. Guess they figured that way none of us inmates could escape.

The back door was a set of air-lock double doors leading out to a small parking lot near the lunchroom. Obviously that parking lot was used only for staff parking and loading supplies.

I had been standing near the back door, staring out at the lot, when the smell hit me. Not the smell of death, or of antiseptic. This smell was of apple cinnamon, mixed with a little spice. And as it drifted over me, I actually felt warm, as if I were in a wonderful kitchen somewhere and apple pies were just coming out of the oven.

I turned around, but there was no one beyond the few residents sitting outside their rooms in their wheelchairs. It seemed that a home policy was to wheel the residents who couldn't walk back to their door after eating, but not inside. Then a while later someone else would come along and put them away.

I suppose the theory being that at least the view in the hall would help break the boredom for the residents. From the looks of most of the residents sitting outside their doors, boredom was the least of their problems.

The wonderful fresh smell of warm cinnamon stayed with me.

With my nose in the air sniffing like a tracking dog, I moved a few steps back into the hall, trying to trace where that wonderful scent was coming from.

When I turned to the right the smell almost vanished, so I quickly moved back and into the left hall. The smell seemed to get stronger and stronger as I moved until finally it surrounded me and a little, shriveled woman sitting in a wheelchair outside her room's door. The sign next to the door on the wall said Rosie Manning,

I walked a few steps past her, but the smell started to fade so I moved back and stood in front of her. She was the source of the smell. Of that there was no doubt, but I couldn't really believe it.

Rosie Manning was a woman of maybe seventy pounds, her back bent over so much that her chin barely stayed above her lap. She seemed to be shaking slightly as she slowly took shallow breaths.

I bent down in front of her and was even more startled. The remains of her dinner covered the bib in her lap and she seemed to be drooling.

And her eyes were blank.

Totally blank.

It was clear that whoever Rosie Manning had been was now long since gone. Only her body was hanging around until something in it decided to stop.

I stood as the nice young orderly who had wheeled me to my room approached.

"I see you've met Rosie," he said, moving around behind her chair. "Afraid she's not real talkative, though. In fact, in the ten years she's been here she's never said a word.

Ten years? I was shocked. "It was her smell," I said, "that made me stop." The thick odor of apples and cinnamon still filled the air like a grandmother's kitchen in the fall.

The young guy wrinkled his nose and took a deep sniff. "I don't smell anything different." He bent over Rosie. "Rosie, did you have an accident in your diaper?"

He shrugged to me as he stood and pushed her into her room. "Guess the nurse's aide will have to check."

I stared after him for a moment, wondering if he had just been pulling my leg. After a few moments the smell started to fade, so reluctantly I headed back for my room, my new home, for my first night's sleep in my new and final bed.

Three

THE SMELL CAME back to me in my dream, seemingly stronger than it had been earlier.

I found myself, in my dream, walking back down the hall of the home, again following the smell. And it led me right back to Rosie's room.

Only this time, her room wasn't the normal nursing home room like mine, but instead was a huge old kitchen full of hanging pans, large pots on the stove, and green trees outside the window over the double sink.

Apples filled a bushel basket on the wooden table and two large pies were cooling on the counter. A small, straight-backed woman worked at the stove, her back to the door as I stared in.

After a moment she turned and smiled. "Come in, my dear," she said. "The pie will be cool enough to eat in a few minutes."

Even knowing it was a dream, I felt hesitant. But the smell was so wonderful that I couldn't stay out in the stark hallway one moment longer. I stepped through the door and was instantly surrounded by warmth and the wonderful smells of cooking. I had never felt so safe and comfortable before.

The woman smiled, wiping her hands on her apron. "I'm Rosie," she said. "Rosie Manning."

She extended her hand and I took it, feeling the firm warm skin in my palm.

"Dorothy," I said, as I shook her hand. "Dorothy McDonald. Dot to my friends."

Rosie smiled. "Rest your feet, Dot." She pointed to an open kitchen chair and I moved to it while she checked on the pies. The door into the kitchen still led back into the hallway of the nursing home and down the hall I could see one of the night nurses working near a cart. But I couldn't hear the nurse.

I would have never recognized that the woman who stood in front of me now in my dream was the same woman who had been a dead hulk in a wheelchair earlier.

"This is a wonderful dream," I said, feeling the top of the wooden table. This kitchen reminded me so much of my own kitchen in my own house. The house my son had sold out from under me.

"Isn't it?" Rosie said as she slid one of the fresh pies onto the table in front of me.

She retreated to the counter and pulled out two plates, a knife, a pie server, and two napkins

"You know this is a dream?" I asked.

"Of course, my dear," she said as she returned and sat down across from me, moving the basket of apples away from her slightly.

I laughed. "I suppose that makes sense. It's my dream, so someone in my dream would know it's a dream."

Rosie laughed too. "You may be right." She expertly sliced the fresh apple pie, sending a warm, wonderful odor filling the air. "But it's my dream too."

I sat back staring at her as she dished up the pie and slid a piece in front of me. I knew this was a dream, yet it felt somehow different. Different in a way that made me want to wake up. Yet the smell of the pie in front of me kept me from pushing myself back to the reality of my small room.

I picked up the fork and took a golden bite of pie.

The taste was even more heavenly than the smell and I felt myself relax into the dream. What could it hurt? It was certainly a better place to be than the small nursing home room that smelled of death.

Four

THE NEXT MORNING my memory told me that in my dream Rosie and I had sat around and talked for hours about all sorts of things we'd done. It seems that up until a stroke knocked her down ten years ago, Rosie had lived a full life as mother and then grandmother. Her husband had been on the city council at times and had died of a heart attack on their third trip to Hawaii.

She had continued to travel until the stroke forced her children to put her in the Home. And the memory of all this conversation in my dream felt real, as if I had actually spent the hours talking to her.

And what really bothered me was that normally I never remembered my dreams.

After breakfast, I went back to my room and to my newly installed phone. It had been the one thing I had insisted my son add into my room. At least this way I could still have a small touch with the outside world. I hadn't expected to want to use it this soon.

One phone call to Emmie, the daughter of my old neighbor, told me what I wanted to know. Emmie worked in records at the county and her mother always told me that Emmie and her computer could find out more about a person than another person had the right to know.

It only took Emmie a minute to tell me that Rosie Manning had indeed been married to Harold Manning, who at one time had served on the city council and later on the planning and zoning commission. He had died fourteen years ago while in Hawaii.

I hung up the phone shocked.

And very much in denial.

Somehow, some way, I must have known Rosie from before her stroke, maybe I had even been in a kitchen like the one in my dream. There was no other explanation.

I made myself focus on the game shows on television until lunch and took a nap until dinner. It felt like a routine I was going to be doing for a very long time to come.

But after dinner, I again found myself walking past Rosie's room. And again I could smell the wonderful odor of cooking around where she sat, her almost dead body hunched over in her chair, the stains of her dinner on her bib.

I stood over her for a moment, my hand resting on the back of her chair. Her thinning white hair barely covered the red, flaky surface of her scalp.

I was almost afraid to go back to my room.

Afraid to lie down and sleep.

Afraid of the pleasant dream I might have. Afraid because I didn't understand what was happening.

Five

THE SECOND DREAM started the same as the first.

I walked down the hall and stood in front of Rosie's door, watching her work at her counter inside a kitchen five times larger than her nursing home room.

This time the smell that filled the air around me was rich with chocolate and vanilla. From where I stood I could see she was mixing up an icing while two halves of a chocolate-layered cake cooled on racks.

She turned and saw me and motioned me to come in. Then she went back to working in the bowl with a small electric hand mixer.

Hesitantly, I moved inside and stood near the wooden table, enjoying the smell and the warmth and watching until she'd finished.

Finally she turned off the mixer, pulled out the beaters, turned and held one up for me. "Just in time to lick off the icing."

I took the one offered and watched as she licked the other, obviously enjoying the task like a kid would have done.

I followed her example and a few moments later found myself working at

getting every lick of the sweet-tasting frosting.

I finished and handed her back the beater. She smiled at me, a fleck of white frosting on her chin. "Glad you came," she said. "I wasn't sure that you would."

"It's just a dream," I said, my voice sounding in my ears a little more insistent than I wanted it to sound. "I didn't have a choice."

She laughed and moved back to put the beaters in the sink. "Of course you do," she said.

I shook my head slowly from side to side as she moved to the cake on the racks. What she had said made no sense to me. "How can you control your dreams?"

She shrugged while testing to see if the cakes were still too hot to frost. They obviously were, so she turned back to me. "I don't know how, but I know I do, ever since I had my stroke." She laughed. "Actually, I did before the stroke, too. Much of my life was like a wonderful dream."

She turned and indicated the full kitchen. "I live in here, now. I really never go out there much at all." She pointed to the door that led into the hall of the nursing home.

I glanced at the darkened hall and then back at her. She was smiling. "Tea?" she asked.

I nodded and she went to work getting out a kettle and filling it with water, then placing it on the stove.

The next morning I remembered when I woke up that we had spent three wonderful hours talking about our lives, our dead husbands, and our children. I remembered I told her what my son had done to me and she shook her head in sadness. "You deserve so much better," she had said.

In the morning I agreed with her even more than I had in the dream. I did deserve better. And so did she.

At breakfast, lunch and dinner I sat with her while the aide fed her a sloppy mush that served as her food. More of it ended up on her bib than in her mouth.

Six

THE THIRD DREAM, she had just finished a steaming hot bowl of popcorn and the smell was so wonderful I almost walked into her kitchen before she invited me in. But luckily she saw me standing there and waved me to the table before I had barged rudely in.

"I already have the water on for tea," she said as I sat down and took a handful of popcorn. In the real world, outside this dream, I would have been hesitant to eat popcorn due to my dentures. But this was a dream and I knew it. And if a person couldn't eat popcorn in a dream, what was the point of dreaming?

She sat down across from me and took a handful of popcorn. Then between bites she said, "I'm going to be moving on tomorrow."

"What?"

"My old body will finally give up tomorrow and I will move on." She shrugged. "Not much I can do about it."

"How do you know?" I managed to ask. For some reason the thought of her not being here in my dreams scared me in a very selfish way.

She shrugged. "I just know. And when your time comes, you'll know, too."

"Since this is my dream, can't I change it?"

She smiled a sad smile at me. "I want to move on. If you were stuck with a body like mine, you would too. Now, let's talk about more pleasant subjects."

At that point, the kettle started to boil and she stood to retrieve it.

For the next three hours we talked and laughed and I forced myself to not talk about what she had told me. And a huge part of me didn't believe her.

The next morning at breakfast I looked for her, but she wasn't there. The head nurse told me that she had died before breakfast.

That night, for the first time since moving into the Home, I didn't dream.

And the next day the smell of death and antiseptic closed in around me like a heavy, smothering blanket.

Seven

IT TOOK ME two days of feeling trapped and smothered before Rosie's words finally sunk all the way in. I did deserve better and unlike her, I might still be able to get it.

With one phone call I reached John, an old friend of my husband.

An old attorney friend.

It took me a good half hour, with him asking pointed questions about my affairs, before I had fully explained everything my son had done and what I hoped John could do for me.

That night I dreamed of a different kitchen. The walls were blank and the counters empty. And there were no smells, but it was a start, because somehow I knew it was my kitchen.

And the wonderful smells would come.

John called me back the next morning and told me he could, with very little work, get my money from the sale of my house out from under my son's name, as well as the rest of my savings. He also told me he'd found a wonderful little cottage with a great kitchen he thought I should see.

That afternoon a real estate agent named Sherry came by and took me to see the house. I should have known it would have the kitchen from my dream, but it still surprised me that it was.

The next day John came by and had me sign papers, including the papers for buying my little house.

By the time my son learned of what I had done, it was finished and he had nothing to say about it.

I had a new home.

That night, my last night in the Home, I dreamed of Rosie again. I dreamed I was standing in her kitchen door and she was smiling at me. Her kitchen smelled of butterscotch pudding and felt warm and welcoming as always. But this time I didn't go in and she didn't invite me. We both knew it wasn't yet my time.

"Come visit me any time," I said to her through the door.

"I just might," she said.

Without me telling her she knew I now had my own home and kitchen, again. And my own life again, something Rosie could never get back for herself after her stroke.

So instead she had built a world and a wonderful kitchen inside her head and lived there.

"You have a wonderful dream," she said, smiling.

I laughed, remembering my own words from days before. "So do you," I said. "Thanks for inviting me in."

She shrugged, the smile never leaving her face. "No need to thank me. It was your dream, too."

I laughed, waved good-bye to her and turned away.

In my dream I walked back to my room, letting the smell of warm butterscotch fade slowly behind me down the dark hall of Shady Hills Nursing Home.

~

Now Available
from all your favorite booksellers
in trade paper and electronic editions.

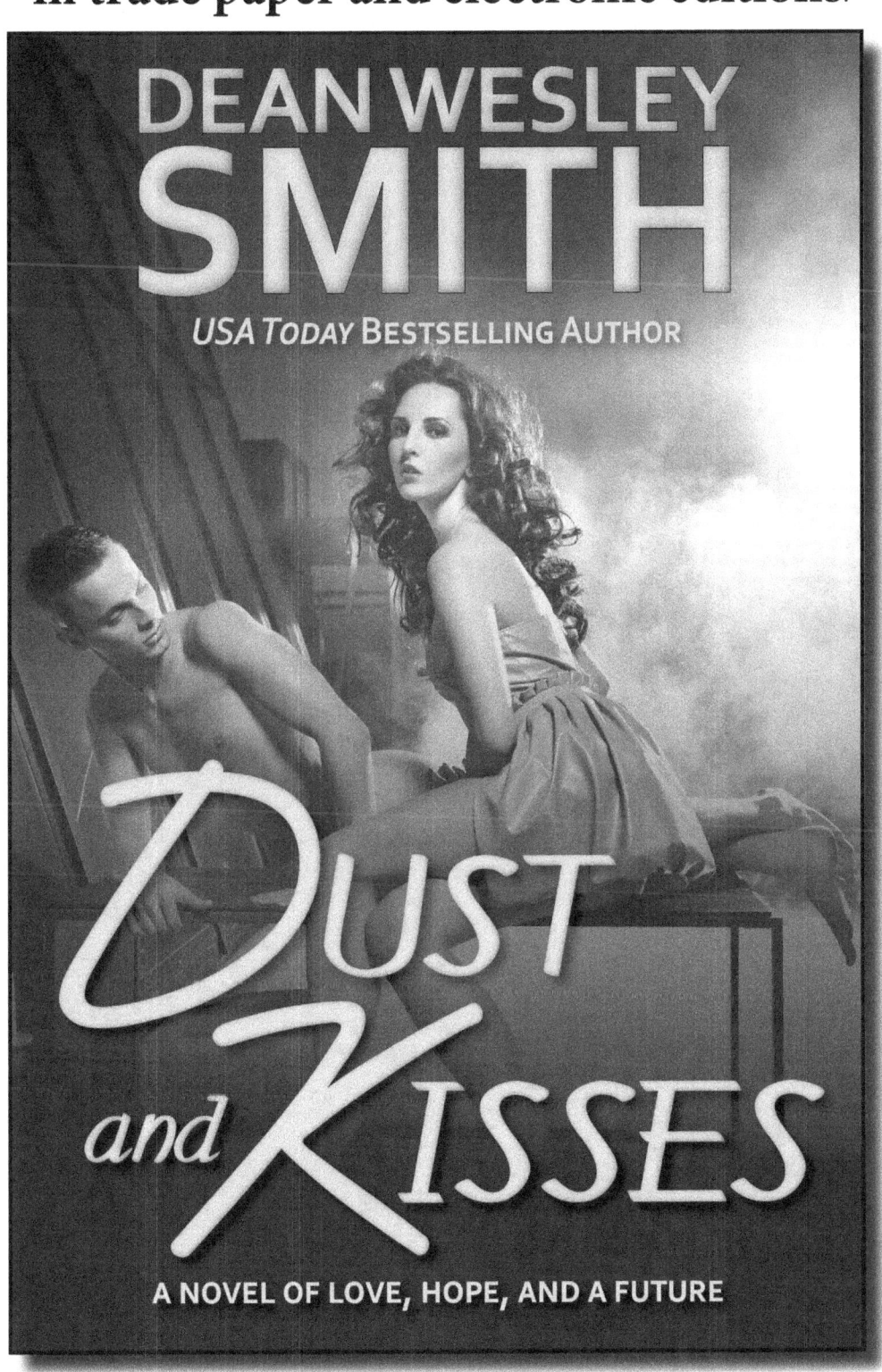

USA Today Bestselling Writer
DEAN WESLEY
SMITH
Music Can
Save You
IN CASE OF EMERGENCY

USA Today bestselling author, Dean Wesley Smith, delves into one of his favorite topics: Music. People always say that music can fix just about anything. Maybe it can.

Titanic Dougherty, one of the biggest and strangests characters to ever walk into a bar clearly believes it can.

Sage, the bartender, isn't so sure.

But in one neighborhood bar, with just regular people, unexplained things can happen when Titanic Dougherty ducks in through the door.

IN CASE OF EMERGENCY

One

MARY JUDE WAS runnin' the drinks and I was makin' them that first night Titanic Dougherty ducked through the door and slid his black leather briefcase up on the bar.

It was a normal early November night at Sandy's, with about twelve regulars scattered around the six wooden tables in the middle and eight booths with lit beer signs over them that ringed the place. The Coors sign over the second booth on the right flickered, so none of the regulars ever sat in that booth.

The evening was still young and even a few of the day-crowd regulars were at the long polished wooden bar.

The place now smelled more of wood polish and spilled beer than it did of smoke, but if you really paid attention, the decades of smoke that clouded in the place still left a faint background hint. I kind of liked it. Reminded me of simpler times.

Sandy's was tucked off to the side of Portland, Oregon, near the river and the shipping docks. From the outside, it was hard to spot because of the big pine trees on both sides and the gravel parking lot that made the cinderblock building tucked back in the trees seem like a long ways from the road.

Plus Jacob hadn't bothered to fix the sign since it got knocked sideways in a windstorm two winters ago, so other than some spotlights on the front of the building, the place was a dark building. At night, no one with a sane mind would come in that front door, yet we seemed to keep a steady stream of customers up, mostly regulars from around the older neighborhood and dock workers.

The sight of Titanic, someone brand new to the bar, stopped everyone in the bar cold, and I figured the shock of seeing someone that big might've even stopped the old juke if Benny, a drunk regular from the day shift, hadn't just plugged it and punched up *She Ain't Pretty But She Don't Snore*, the most obnoxious song to ever blare out a speaker.

My name's George Armstrong Sage. Everyone calls me Sage. I've been the bartender here at Sandy's Lounge since Jacob, the owner, got shot by a wild-eyed kid trying to get enough money for his next fix.

Jacob survived, but hasn't done much bartending since. That was three years ago and I've seen some strange happenings in all those nights, but nothing comes close to Titanic Dougherty and that black briefcase of his.

Describing Titanic ain't no easy chore. Let me put it this way, I'm no short drift at six-four, and most don't give me shit since I weigh in at over two-eighty.

I got a face that spent its time being hit by football players and baseball players and shoulders that hint at my days of playing ball. But standing next to Titanic, I'd look like that damn doughboy they show bouncing around on those commercials.

Titanic was one big son of a bitch.

That first time Titanic ducked through the front door, he was decked out completely in black, right up to one of the only black baseball caps I've ever seen. The black, tent-sized sweatshirt he wore had the number two on both shoulders and the huge muscles in his legs stretched his jeans.

I figured he might have played for a team somewhere, but I didn't recognize him. That didn't mean much since I spent my time at first base for a few years for a few teams and no one recognizes me.

"Double scotch," he said, carefully pushing the business-looking briefcase to one side. "Rocks, splash soda."

His deep-voiced request finally jolted me enough to get me to close my mouth and quit staring.

He swiveled around on his stool and glared at the other dozen or so who were silently gaping at him.

I don't know who would have won that stand-off, him or the regular customers, if the words of the song hadn't broke the tension.

...with sharp-edged curlers and flannel to the floor,
thank God, Mother, at least she don't snore.

Slowly, Titanic turned, looked at the jukebox, and then smiled.

The smile grew until he started to laugh a deep, glass-shaking laugh. That got everyone else laughing and talking.

I scrambled to the well and fixed him a solid double scotch, like he ordered, and slid it in front of him as he turned back to face the bar.

He pulled out his black leather wallet, fumbled in it with huge fingers and then pulled out a twenty and shoved it toward me. "Thanks," he said. "Hold on to that and let me know when you need more."

By the time I had rang up his drink and fixed a few for Mary Jude to take out to the lovebirds in the back booth, Mary Jude was looking at Titanic sort of glassy-eyed.

And Titanic was ready for another.

I slid the second one up beside the first. "This one's on me," I said and stuck out my hand. "Sage is what they call me."

"Thanks, Mr. Sage," he said, gripping my hand with a solid grasp that made me feel like a child shaking hands with an adult. No one had ever really done that to me before.

"They call me Titanic. Titanic Dougherty."

Much to my relief, he let go of my hand and picked up his drink. The glass looked like a child's cup in his hand. "Nice place you got here," he said. "Yours?"

"Nope. I'm just the regular hired help."

He nodded kind of slow and sipped on his drink.

"You pick the songs?" He motioned toward the jukebox.

I laughed. "Are you kidding? Some curly headed kid from Bently's Music services the thing. He comes in during the afternoons about once every two weeks. Worst songs I've ever heard."

Titanic laughed his rumbling laugh. "I'll agree with you on that. Maybe, just maybe, I might be able to fix that."

He patted the briefcase and then downed the rest of his drink and slid it toward me for a refill.

At that point I figured he was some sort of music salesman.

Mary Jude come up right about then with a long list of drinks. Seems Titanic had made a few people nervous so they had to down their drinks.

I didn't have time to ask him what he actually did after I refilled his drink.

When I finally did have the time, he started asking me questions instead and I found myself telling him all about my ex-wife, Rita, and how she, without meaning to, had pushed me to try to become rich to the point where I no longer could stand the pressure.

I told him about how I once had played pro baseball and loved it more than anything.

I even ended up telling him why I was bartending instead of working as an electrical engineer like I had trained for in college.

He also asked Mary Jude a bunch about herself and I found myself listening and learning more about her than I had known after six months of working with her.

Hell, I didn't even realize that she had been married and had two kids living with her ex-husband and his new wife in Alaska. She said she hadn't seen them in half a year and probably wouldn't until summer.

She told Titanic all about how lonely she was and about her studio apartment and about how she never dated because the only time she ever met anyone was at work.

Boy, I understood that about this place. Once you knew the regulars, there was no one here to interest her or me, for that matter.

After a half hour, I found myself looking at her and not seeing Mary Jude, the cocktail waitress, but Mary Jude, the person.

An amazing transformation.

It was funny how that big guy could draw information out of people.

He left that night after drinking seventeen dollars of the twenty and leaving me the rest. I realized later that I knew nothing more about him than I had the moment he came in.

Two

HE DUCKED BACK in the front door two nights later at nine o'clock. Like the first time, everyone stared, but after a second, a few waved hello. He had on a white sweatshirt this time, Levis, and a red baseball cap with the word "Davis" across the top.

Again, he carried the black leather briefcase.

He slid the briefcase up on the bar and took the stool next to old Richard Butler. Richard was one of the regulars who worked down at the docs and drank his supper every night.

Usually Richard was gone by nine with six or seven bourbon-waters under his belt.

For some reason, tonight he had stayed late and was still in his normal spot at the bar.

"A little better music this time," Titanic said as I slid the bar napkin in front of him and he flipped a twenty at me. Someone had punched up a country song, but not a person in the bar was paying attention to it. I wouldn't have noticed if Titanic hadn't said something. I guess I only heard the bad ones.

"You like music, huh?" old Richard said, looking up from the bottom of his last drink.

"Same?" I asked Titanic, picking up the twenty.

Titanic nodded, then turned to Richard. "Don't you?"

Old Richard shook his head side to side in a drunken exaggerated motion.

"Naw. My son liked the stuff and it drove me to drink." He picked up his empty glass and tried to get something more out of it while chuckling to himself.

I headed down the bar toward the well to make Titanic's drink and by the time I got back, Titanic had old Richard telling him all about his son and about how he was killed on a music field trip while still in high school. Hell, I'd been serving Richard for three years and not once had he mentioned he'd had a son.

Or that the son had died.

For the rest of that evening, I watched Titanic get people who got near him at the bar to talk about themselves and about their lives and their loves without once mentioning one thing about himself.

I think he knew I was watching him, because every so often he would look up at me and point over at the jukebox and say, "Interesting song. Listen to the words."

Then he'd go back to whatever conversation he was having at the time.

That instruction from him always brought the song out loud and clear as if it hadn't been playing the moment before. Usually the words would mean something to me, or get me remembering a part of my life with Rita, or something about my work or my ball-playing days.

Again Titanic stayed for seventeen dollars of his twenty and like he had the first time, left without a word about himself ever being said.

Three

AFTER THAT HE started coming in twice a week.

Mondays and Thursdays. He always dressed comfortably and always had the black leather briefcase with him. He became another of the regulars, accepted by most of the old-timers as if he'd been around for years instead of weeks.

I loved that about bars like Sandy's. Once you were in, you were accepted, no matter how strange you looked or what you did or didn't do outside of Sandy's.

It was the Thursday night during his third week that I finally got up enough courage to ask him what he did with the briefcase. I did it real casual-like as I slid a drink in front of him and I think I almost caught him off guard.

Almost.

He paused for a long second, looking at me, then he smiled and patted the case lightly with one big hand. "I use it for emergencies."

"How's that?"

He pointed a finger up in the air. "Notice the song? Good message in this one."

The old Kenny Rodgers' song blared over my consciousness like someone had turned up the volume. Without thinking I found myself following the words as I walked back toward the well.

When I turned around, Titanic had picked up his drink and joined a group over in the corner, leaving his briefcase and his money sitting in their normal spot on the bar.

About a month after Titanic started coming into Sandy's, Mary Jude started having troubles.

The only reason I noticed it was because Titanic started talking to her a bunch more and I overheard some of her problems. It seemed the loneliness was getting to her and her ex-husband was being a real bastard about letting her see the kids. She just couldn't afford to fly up to Alaska or help fly them down.

It looked as if she might not even get to see them this summer and that had her awful depressed.

I noticed one Tuesday she came in for work with her eyes red.

I asked her if there was anything I could do, but she just shook her head. That night Titanic came in and talked to her and she seemed to be a lot better by the end of the night.

But she was back depressed again the next night.

The following Monday she didn't show for work.

Titanic came in at nine and he didn't look happy. He sat his black briefcase down on the bar and looked over at me. "Mary Jude?"

"Didn't come in," I said. "I tried to call her, but didn't get an answer."

He nodded. "She is one very sick woman and there doesn't seem to be much more I can do to help her." He stood with both huge hands on the case and stared down at it as if it might explode at any moment.

"Help her?" I asked. "You a doctor?"

He looked up at me and smiled that same smile adults give kids when they ask a reasonable question that seems to have an obvious other answer. "No, I'm not," he said. "I am a musician. And I think it may be time I play my latest song."

He clicked open the latches on the briefcase and opened the case. The sound of those latches clicking shocked the bar into silence.

Inside, the case was lined in a black velvet and completely empty except for one forty-five record in a paper slip.

He carefully picked up the forty-five and closed the case.

"May I play this on your jukebox?"

I stared at the record for a moment, then looked up at him. "I don't have a key."

"I can open it."

"Then be my guest," I said.

I didn't know what to think. One moment we were talking about Mary Jude and how sick she was and the next he tells me the first bit of information I've heard about him, then opens up a case he's brought with him every night and pulls out a stupid record.

He moved over to the jukebox and with a movement of his hand that I couldn't follow, had the top up. He studied the insides for a moment, then inserted his record carefully. At this point, not only was I watching him, but so was everyone in the place.

He closed the top of the jukebox and turned back to face me.

"I'm sorry for what this will do to you. And to all of you."

He swept his arm around to include everyone in the bar. At that moment there were about twenty of the regulars scattered around, most of them he had talked to at one point or another.

"It is better people learn their lessons without help," he said, his big rumbling voice filling the silence of Sandy's. "But I feel Mary Jude may be in danger and I must try to help her."

He patted the jukebox. "And this is the only way I know how."

"Just exactly what are you planning on doing?" I asked.

"I'm just going to play my latest song," he said. "Nothing more."

With that, he turned to the jukebox and punched two buttons. Right at that point you could hear the traffic outside on the distant street that ran in front of the bar.

No one said a word.

The song started low, almost as if it really didn't have one starting point but had always been there below the level of hearing. I think the instrument was a flute, but someone later said they'd heard a guitar.

All I know is that when it started, I suddenly felt light-headed.

And when the words started with the sound of Titanic's voice, deep and full and rich, I felt the room spin.

Titanic slowly faded away, as if his massive frame had never been standing there.

Everyone agreed later that he had disappeared.

Or at least everyone thought they saw him disappear.

And everyone agreed that after a few seconds, he was back, dancing with Mary Jude.

I remember half watching them dance, his huge frame agile and light as he led her in and out of the tables. She was smiling and radiant, staring up at his face.

But the other half of me was years away from Sandy's Bar, drifting over my past decisions and events of my life as smoothly as Titanic and Mary Jude drifted past the tables in Sandy's Lounge.

I saw clearly what I had done right and where I had been wrong.

I understood for the first time why Rita had pushed me so hard.

By the end of the song, I finally understood what I needed to do to be happy with myself.

How I had been only hiding in Sandy's.

Everything.

As the last notes of the music died into the walls and the wooden tables and the beer signs, Mary Jude and Titanic faded away as if someone had turned a fan on a cloud of smoke.

And the silence that followed lasted one damn long time.

Four

JACOB LOST MORE than half of his regular customers that night, as Titanic's song changed their lives as it changed mine.

But not a one of us could remember the words to his song.

Or the tune.

We just remember listening to it. And what that listening did to each of us.

Jacob told me that Mary Jude had called him and quit. She had said she was going back to Alaska to fight for her kids like she should have done the first time.

No one ever saw Titanic again, and we couldn't find his record anywhere in the jukebox.

Two weeks later, I quit tending bar at Sandy's to take a job as a scout for the local semi-pro baseball team. It was a start back, a start to a new life of not hiding.

Titanic's black briefcase was still sitting behind the bar the day I left, as empty as I had been before he had played his most recent song.

I patted it on the way out and said, "Thanks."

~

DEAN WESLEY SMITH

THE LIFE AND TIMES OF

BUFFALO JIMMY

Chapters 22-24

What Came Before...

Nineteen-year-old Boston native Jimmy Gray had been traveling with his parents and older brother, Luke, headed west to find a new home and new riches. Before even reaching Independence, they were attacked and robbed by Jake Benson and his gang. Jimmy's parents were killed, his brother wounded.

In one of the wildest towns in all of American history, Jimmy Gray, a sheltered, educated son of a banker from Boston suddenly finds himself very, very much alone. But then through some luck, he finds other young men about his age and down on their luck who might be able to help him.

Together, the five of them head west after Benson. They end up hunting buffalo as he always dreamed of doing, but then they are hit with a massive flash flood and Jimmy is left alone, his friends more than likely dead. Luckily, they all meet up again and are all safe. So they continue west, knowing that Benson is just ahead of them.

Suddenly they come upon Benson and his men killing a farm family. They manage to get one of the men separated from the others, but in a fall he accidently dies. So they scatter to meet up later at a camp. They managed that but found a survivor of the killings. So one of them had to go back with the kid while the others followed Benson.

They caught him once again terrorizing a small wagon train and managed to scare him and his men off.

THE LIFE AND TIMES OF BUFFALO JIMMY

Part Twenty-Two
HEADED TOWARD DANGER

MORE THAN THREE weeks had passed since Zach and Truitt had rejoined them from taking the young boy back. It had been the longest and hottest three weeks Jimmy could ever remember. They had followed slowly, very slowly, behind the wagon train that Benson and his men were shadowing.

Long reported that one of Benson's men, the one with the broken arm, seemed to be getting weaker and weaker, which got a cheer from everyone. It had been C.J., with his special sling, that had hit the man in the arm with a rock.

They were all proud of the fact that they had rescued an entire wagon company from Benson and his killers. To Jimmy, after not being in time to save the family at the homestead, saving the fine people of that wagon company had felt wonderful.

The people of the company had been very appreciative as well, wanting the boys to ride along with them the rest of the way to California.

Even though there were some pretty girls Jimmy's age with the company, all of them had decided to move on, to stay close behind Benson and his men.

The trail across most of Northern Nevada wound in and out of the desert scrub and rocks beside the ever-smaller flow of the Humboldt River. They had had to cross the river seven times, but the flow was so small, the crossings hadn't ever been a problem.

As C.J. and Josh had told them, ahead was the Humboldt Sink, where what was left of the river just vanished into desert.

And beyond that, the hardest leg of the trip, the Forty Mile Desert.

Every day along the Humboldt, the temperatures were unbearable in the afternoon, so they had adopted a travel method of getting up before dawn and moving in the early light, then by noon finding a shelter of either brush or rocks and resting during the hot hours.

Long kept great care of their horses, making sure they were fed and watered the right amounts, but even with the good care and decent grass, the heat was clearly taking a toll on them. A week earlier, Long had shifted the horse C.J. was riding to a pack horse because it couldn't carry C. J.'s weight and his gear anymore.

Along the river, Jimmy was stunned at how many broken-down wagons littered the trail. At each wagon without people, Jimmy had them search for water bags and smaller supplies that might come in handy. They had found a few water bags and a canteen.

With what Jimmy understood they were facing, trying to carry extra water might just be what saved their lives.

Years and years of dead stock bones, bleached white, littered the sides of the trail as well. There weren't that many wagon companies ahead of them yet this summer, since they were traveling by horse, but even so, there were already dozens of fresh dead animals beside the trail, most of them torn apart by packs of wild dogs Josh said were called coyotes.

Jimmy couldn't imagine what it was going to be like when all the wagons behind them got here, in the heat of August. The entire trail would smell like death almost every step of the way.

They had had to pass at least four solo wagons with families. They had broken down and been left by their companies who had had no choice but to move on.

They had stopped to see if they could help at each family, but there was really nothing they could do. The families all seemed to have water and food. Jimmy figured that with luck, the families would join up with another company coming along, either with their wagon fixed or walking the rest of the way. Otherwise, if at some point they didn't move forward, those families, children and all, would just die in the extreme heat of the desert.

As each day went by, and the farther they got down the Humboldt, the more graves there were, all with names roughly scratched into wooden crosses.

Josh started to write down all the names and locations, but after a week on the Humboldt, there were so many, he gave up the task as too depressing.

Two days away from the Humboldt Sink, Josh read them all a passage from his favorite writer, Mark Twain, who had been out west a few years earlier and had written about the Forty Mile Desert.

Twain said, "It would hardly be an exaggeration to say that we could have walked the forty miles and set our feet on a bone at every step."

"Okay, no more of that," Truitt said, shaking his head. "We still have to cross that thing."

With the intense heat, all the bones and graves along the Humboldt, and forty miles of sand ahead of them, Jimmy could imagine Twain being very, very right about what they were facing.

Jimmy sure wasn't looking forward to that leg on this adventure.

Part Twenty-three
KNOWING WHAT'S AHEAD

THE WAGON COMPANY that Benson was following camped for three days on the edge of the Sink, so they were forced to camp back down the trail a half-day's ride to make sure they weren't seen.

Just sitting, not moving, bothered Jimmy more than anything. But Long said it was a good thing, since they were resting the horses, and gaining all their strength before crossing the Forty Mile Desert.

With the wagon company camped like that, Long was able to get much clos-

er. It seemed, from what Long overheard, that some of the men of the company had died during a river crossing early in the trip, and now there were only five men and three older boys in the seven wagons, with a dozen young children and ten women.

Long said Benson and his men were pretending they were going to help the company across the desert.

"Not likely," Jimmy had said. "It's only a matter of time before those people meet a very sad end."

"Unless we can do something to stop Benson," Josh said.

"I'm open to any ideas," Jimmy said.

They talked about it for most of the evening and all of the next day, but no one could come up with anything that would allow them to stop Benson and not get killed.

The wagon company was camped right out in the open, above the water, with no place around the wagon camp to surprise Benson with any kind of attack. And at night, the company had two men standing guard at all times. Usually one of them was one of Benson's men, or Benson himself.

Finally, they all agreed to try to warn one of the men of the wagon company when he got away from the train. It was the best plan they could think of.

Jimmy and Long, just before dawn on the second morning, met one of the younger men from the train while he was out trying to gather wood for a fire. He wasn't much older than they were, and looked very tired and worn out. His clothes were tattered and he looked underfed. Fighting wagons along this trail could do that to a man.

After they had told him about Benson and his two men, the guy had only nodded. "Thanks for the warning, but we don't trust them either. We won't let them get the drop on us." He patted the six-shooter he had tucked into his belt.

"If you need our help, we're camped back down the trail," Jimmy said.

The guy nodded. "We won't. Thanks again, though."

"Just don't tell Benson we're behind you," Jimmy said.

"Oh, trust me," the man had said with a shake of his head, "I don't even talk to those men."

With that, he walked back toward the wagon company carrying an armload of sticks.

Jimmy had no doubt that the warning wouldn't help. If Benson followed his true nature, that man would be dead very shortly.

But there was nothing he or the rest of them could do, so they went back to waiting.

Jimmy wasn't so sure how rested they were getting in the extreme heat. The air just seemed to take any energy he had out of his body, and it wasn't until long after the sun went down and the air cooled that he even started to feel like moving at all.

One night, around the campfire, Josh and C. J. filled them all in on what was coming for them in the desert.

"Most companies start across the desert at night," Josh said, "leaving the camp near the Sink to cross the fifteen miles that it takes to even reach the drop down into the Forty Mile Desert."

"It's well over fifty miles from the last water to the Truckee River," C. J. said.

Together, they all worked out a plan.

Jimmy hadn't liked the sound of anything that was coming.

Fifty-five miles in sand, without water.

They were going to have to be very, very ready for the crossing.

Finally, coming back just after dawn on the third morning, Long reported that the wagon company, with Benson and his men helping them, had started to make the crossing. "They left one wagon behind," Long said, "but no people."

"We go tonight," Jimmy said. "Let's move up to their old camp and get ready. That will give them a full day's head start. We don't want to catch them somewhere out there in the middle of that sand."

"Good idea," Truitt said. "They won't be stopping, that's for sure."

"Neither will we," C.J. said. "Stopping in that desert is the quickest way to die."

"Sounds like a good time," Zach said, shaking his head.

"Before we leave," Jimmy said, "we need to make sure every water bag is full, every canteen."

"I'll have the stock well watered," Long said. "But we're going to need every drop we don't drink for the horses to get them across as well. And we'll have to pack extra grass."

When they reached the campsite beside the sink, they could clearly see the six wagons kicking up dust far out on a vast open expanse of light brown sand.

They found shelter under some trees and settled in.

For Jimmy, the heat of the day seemed to drag on and on.

California was just over those mountains in the distance. Somewhere, between here and Sacramento, he needed to get his father's gold mine deed back from Benson.

He just didn't know how yet.

All of them tried to stay in the shade as long as the sun was out, and from where Jimmy was sitting, by mid-afternoon, he could no longer see the dust trail from the wagons.

Tomorrow, instead of resting in the shade, they would be moving in the heat. Once you started across the desert, there was no stopping.

A lot of things had happened on the trip west, but right now, what faced them frightened him more than anything had frightened him before.

But they had no choice.

If they stopped, they died.

Part Twenty-four
STARTING ACROSS HELL

AS AN ALMOST full moon came up over the hot desert, they broke camp. Every canteen, every water bag was brimming full. Then, with each of them taking one last, long drink from the fresh water near the camp, they started off.

"Stay between the wagon wheel ruts," Long said, taking the lead as he usually did. "Safer in the dark."

Jimmy was last in line and was leading one packhorse.

Zach led another packhorse behind Long.

Then it was C.J., Josh, and Truitt in that order.

They kept close to each other and after a while Jimmy noticed that his eyes had adjusted and he could see pretty well in just the light from the moon.

They moved steadily.

As the night got cooler, Long had them pick up the pace. They needed to cover as much ground as possible when it was cool and dark.

They made the fifteen miles to the edge of the desert without any problems. The moon was directly over their heads as they reached the edge of the Forty Mile Desert.

They stopped for a few minutes rest on the top of the ridge before dropping down the steep incline to the desert floor.

At first, Jimmy didn't understand what he was seeing. The trail was framed all the way down the slope to the level desert floor with piles and piles of white.

Then it suddenly dawned on him what he was actually looking at.

Bones.

Thousands of animals' bones lined both sides of the trail down the hill like a horrid decoration of a nightmarish garden path.

"Ready?" he asked everyone, tearing his gaze away from the bones.

"Not really," C.J. said.

"We've come this far," Truitt said, "we can't let forty miles of sand stop us."

"One at a time down this slope," Long said, mounting up and starting down between the rows of white animal bones gleaming in the moonlight.

Long made it to the bottom fine, and so did Zach with his pack horse.

Truitt went next, then Josh, both signaling they were at the bottom with a whistle.

Jimmy sat on his horse at the top, watching C. J.

Everything seemed to be going fine until suddenly, about halfway down, C.J.'s horse stumbled and went down, dumping C.J. into the deep sand.

C.J. rolled down the hill and came up spitting sand.

Long and Zach, on foot, quickly climbed back up to him while Jimmy led his horses down slowly from the top.

C.J. was fine, but his horse had broken a leg.

They got the supplies and water off the horse and distributed to the other horses. Then C.J., with Long's help, saddled their best packhorse with his gear.

The horse with the broken leg had been one Jimmy's father had bought in St. Louis. For some reason, it suddenly felt as if he was going to lose another member of his family.

He felt sick.

As Jimmy watched, and Long turned his back, Zach did the hardest job he had ever had to do.

He led the horse over to where there was a large pile of white bones that were piled almost waist high.

Then, with one clean shot from the rifle, he put the suffering horse down.

Just like with much of what they had had to do on this trip, there just wasn't a choice.

It was life, or it was death.

And to Jimmy, here in the Wild West, there didn't seem to be much between the two.

Continued next month...

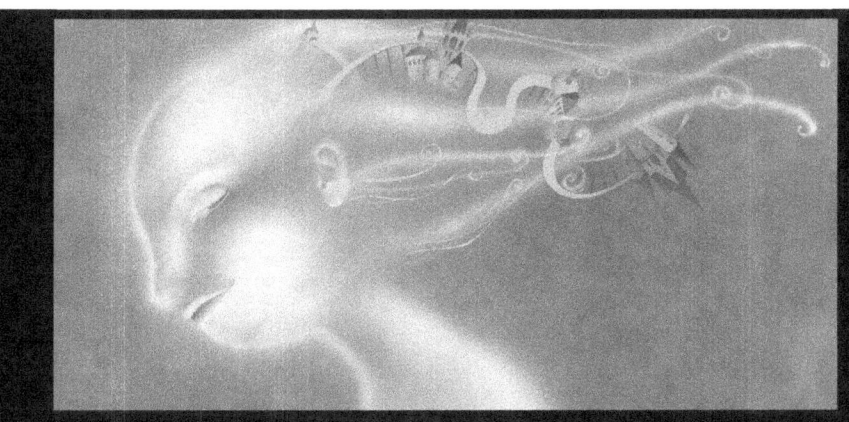

Poems by DEAN WESLEY SMITH

Little Death

She is the only person I know
who would jump from a warm bed,
go down one flight of stairs to the door,
in bright light,
and call her dog
without clothes on.

Across the street an old man
sits wrapped in a shawl
made forty years earlier by his first wife,
eyes circled with bathtub rings
from the binoculars he has held
watching my door waiting for her.

He has been sitting there for twenty-six years.
She is twenty-five.
Naked, she stretches,
hands at mouth,
legs apart,
calling her dog.

He feels an old warmth.
One hand holds the glasses tight,
his other hand fumbles,
grasps the old revolver.
She laughs, turns,
a flash of white back up the stairs.

I watch her approach, complaing of the cold,
laughing at her dog.
I feel an old warmth.
She moves to smother me.
The shot rings out, unnoticed.
She kills us both simultaneously.

DEAN WESLEY SMITH

THE
13TH FLOOR PROBLEM

A POKER BOY STORY

USA Today *bestselling writer once more returns to his favorite character, Poker Boy.*

Poker Boy and his team must figure out why the 13th floors of every major building in Las Vegas were about to disappear. Was it magic? Was it an evil plan to destroy Las Vegas? And who had the power to do such a thing?

One of the more puzzling mysteries that Poker Boy must solve. And he does it in his normal strange and funny way: He asks stupid questions.

This story originally appeared in Fiction River: Hex in the City *and is part of my monthly focus to let readers of this magazine read some of my stories from WMG Publishing's other main publication.*

THE 13th FLOOR PROBLEM
A Poker Boy Story

One

AS A PROFESSIONAL poker player, I don't have any superstitions. Not a one. I don't believe that if I won a tournament with one sock inside out, that I needed to always wear one sock inside out for good luck. I know for a fact that Lady Luck, actually named Laverne, paid no attention at all to how my socks were worn, or if I threw salt over my shoulder, or if I walked under a ladder.

She was just too busy. Now don't take me wrong, I wouldn't want to cross her, but she just wasn't the type to pay attention to the small stuff.

In life and in poker, I have had my fair share of good luck and bad luck, even though as Poker Boy, I know Lady Luck likes me, and my team. In fact, one of her four daughters, Terri, the Queen of Clubs, has just joined my team of superheroes.

My team works to save the world when it needs saving and it is often Lady Luck who gives us the assignments.

As it happened, just luck or coincidence or whatever, most of my team was having lunch in my office when we learned about what we came to call "The 13th Floor Problem."

My office, actually it's my team's office, but everyone calls it my office, floats about five hundred feet above the top floor of MGM Grand Hotel and Casino. It has windows on all four sides, floor-to-ceiling, with a view that was worth more than I wanted to ever imagine.

How it stayed in position was beyond me, even though Stan said I was the one who put it there and kept it there. As far as I was concerned, it stayed in place by some sort of magic I didn't understand. There were a lot of things in the world of gods and superheroes that I didn't understand and how my office worked was one of those things.

The office was, of course, invisible, and, as Stan said, out of phase with the real world so that if a plane hit it, the plane would pass right through. I'm sure if that happened, it would give everyone in the office a heart attack. The last thing I wanted was a plane passing through me.

But the office did have a wonderful view of the Strip and the airport and the entire city around it. Patty Ledgerwood (aka Front Desk Girl and my girlfriend and sidekick) and I often came up here at night and sat together and watched the stars and the planes landing and the cars on the Strip and all the bright lights spread out below us. As I said, a view worth more than I can imagine.

I had decorated the office so it looked like an exact replica of the 1960's diner booth the team used to meet in. The Diner, as the place is called, is in the downtown Vegas area on a side street a block from the Horseshoe Casino and Hotel.

Just as in the Diner downtown, this booth had slick, red seats on three sides. I had added wooden chairs that could be pulled up to the end of the booth and a couple tall, tree-like plants behind the booth to give the place a little less cold feel.

The booth filled most of the room and could seat eight in a pinch.

There were only three ways to get up to the office. I had put a door leading to Patti's apartment and another door leading to the Diner in downtown Vegas. You step through and you were instantly in the other place. Otherwise you had to teleport.

I could teleport, but besides Stan, the God of Poker and my boss, I was the only one on the team who could. Everyone else either hitched a ride here with me or Stan or used the door from the Diner.

I was told it was rare that a lowly superhero like me could teleport. Or step between instants of time. But I had learned how to do both. I figured if I could learn it, so could other superheroes, like my girlfriend, Patty. She was a superhero working in hotel hospitality area of the Gods.

She was willing to learn, so we had worked on it a few times, so far without luck. But we had time and one of Patty's superhero traits was extreme patience. She had to have that to put up with me at times. I was a professional poker player, after all.

It had become a habit for the team to have lunch together in my office around the big booth at one in the afternoon. We all liked the view and the companionship. Sometimes being a superhero could get lonely, at least that's what others told me. As a poker player, I always had people around me. It was part of the job.

And I was lucky enough to be tangled up with Patty.

Screamer and his wife, Terri, were sitting at the table working on burgers and vanilla shakes that Madge from the Diner had brought up. Having the great food and milkshakes from the Diner in downtown Vegas just a step through a door away was a great benefit.

Screamer had been a member of the team since we started. He was a superhero working with the police and could, with a touch, connect minds and be inside another person's mind. He got his nickname Screamer from making hardened criminals scream in fear from the images he put in their heads.

Terri was Lady Luck's daughter and a superhero in the beverage side of things. She and Screamer had been separated for a number of years while he got his newly acquired brain-reading powers under control. Now that they had worked out a way to be together, they never seemed to be apart.

Patty worked at the MGM Grand front desk and was on lunch break, so she still had on her front desk outfit and her long, brown hair pulled back tight. She nibbled at a salad while I worked at a cheeseburger with a huge basket of fries. I had switched away from my standard vanilla milkshake today for a cherry Diet Coke. Patty was mixing my fries with her salad, taking a bite of lettuce, then a fry.

Stan, the God of Poker, and my boss, also had a cheeseburger. He had on his standard tan slacks, tan shirt, and tan vest. He was the most nondescript man I had ever met. You could almost look right at him and not notice him. That made him downright scary on a poker table.

Having Lady Luck herself just come to have lunch with you was a stunning thing I would never get over.

I had just taken a huge bite of my cheeseburger when Laverne, Lady Luck herself, appeared, pulled up a chair, sat at the booth, and grabbed one of my fries. Between her and Patty, I was going to be lucky to get any of them.

Laverne wore her normal gray silk business pants suit and had her hair pulled back tight, giving her face a stark beauty and sternness. She just radiated power and toughness.

And not once being around her did I fail to get nervous. Having Lady Luck herself just come to have lunch with you was a stunning thing I would never get over.

"Hey, Mom," Terri said, working at her hamburger and leaning against Screamer.

I managed to get most of the ketchup off my chin and nodded to her. Stan just kept working on his cheeseburger.

Madge appeared out of the door from the diner and smiled at Laverne. "Anything I can get for you?"

Madge was the waitress and the owner of the Diner downtown. She was also a superhero in the food and beverage industry and seemed to have been around the world of the gods for a very long time. She was fairly short and clearly overweight and she always wore a dress far, far too tight and too short for someone her size. She had a gruff way about her, but was always willing to help out the team where she could. She knew everyone, which had helped a few times on different assignments we had tackled.

Laverne shook her head. "Thanks, Madge, but we have a problem we need to get started on."

I swallowed the last of the bite of my cheeseburger I had been chewing on and pushed the rest away. When Laverne came looking for us like this, it meant eating was going to take a back seat very quickly.

Besides, my stomach was already twisting from my sense of looming danger, so putting more food down there wasn't a good idea at the moment.

"What's happening?" Stan asked, then took another bite of his cheeseburger.

"All the thirteenth floors are vanishing," Laverne said, as if she said a statement like that every day.

Then she took another fry.

"No building or hotel in this city has a thirteenth floor," Terri said, looking puzzled.

"Floor Twelve B or the Fourteenth Floor, whatever they are called," Laverne said, shrugging. "They are all vanishing. They will still be there, so no building is going to fall down, but the floors will become totally invisible by midnight."

"The Magician is back," Madge said, shaking her head and sighing in a way I had never heard before.

"Maybe," Laverne said, taking one more fry. She gave me that serious stare that scared me down to my very toes. "And if The Magician is behind this in any way, we need to stop him. And quickly."

At that, she vanished with one of my French fries in her hand.

The stunned silence around the office matched how I felt.

I just wish I had a clue what was happening.

And how she seemed to know something that was going to happen in two days.

And who the hell The Magician was.

Two

EVERYONE had stopped eating.

Terri was just shaking her head, her long black hair going back and forth around her face.

Madge was frowning, never a good sign when a waitress used to attempting to smile was frowning.

Stan looked angry and Patty looked confused, just as I was feeling.

"Time for milkshakes," Madge said.

At that moment every bit of food on the table vanished and Madge turned and stepped through the door back to the Diner.

The group had a habit of ordering milkshakes when we were working on a problem. Usually only big problems. So Madge thought this problem big enough for milkshakes and had cleared the table.

Again not a good sign.

I stared at the place on the booth where my French fries had been and kind of wished I had the power to bring them back. And then I wondered where they had gone, and then finally decided I didn't want to know any of those details. Not at the moment, anyway.

I glanced around at my team, then decided that none of them were going to speak, so it was up to me to be my normal clueless self and ask dumb questions. Sometimes my dumb questions got to the heart of the problem facing us, sometimes they just made me look silly for asking.

I wanted to start with how someone knew what was going to happen two days in the future, but decided on something more basic. "So someone want to give me the background on The Magician?"

"Right now he goes by Nick Scipio," Stan said without looking up. "He's been around for longer than anyone knows for certain. The protector and father, basically, of modern magic. Over the centuries he's taken many names when free, from Dedi in Egypt to Robert-Houdin."

"Is he a god?" Patty asked.

"He's an elf," Stan said.

I moaned. We had dealt a number of times with the elves and trolls and their fights. Because I had caught the one person causing elves and trolls to always battle, I was honored in their hidden casino here in Vegas, but I seldom went there. Just often enough to not insult them by never going there.

"You said something about him being free?" Screamer asked, and Terri nodded beside him, her black hair moving around her face.

"He is sort of locked up in a time cell," Stan said, "between moments of time, that should make it impossible for him to escape. But he often does. It's been a good fifty years since his last escape, at least that I heard about."

"So why make all the 13th floors disappear?" I asked.

"You could ask him yourself," Madge said, appearing from the doorway of the Diner carrying six milkshakes.

Behind her strolled a tall, thin man with black hair covering the tips of his pointed ears. He wore a white frilly shirt like he was on the way to a wedding and a long, black cape. In one hand he carried a cane, but clearly didn't need it.

"I figured Madge would know where you all met," he said, his voice low and soothing in an odd way.

He looked around at the view, clearly impressed, then he stopped in front of the booth and bowed slightly. "The Magician at your service. And I want to be very clear that I will have nothing to do with the building floors disappearing in just under two days. But I must admit, it's a nice bit. I kind of wish I had thought of it."

He pulled up a chair and sat on it, facing all of us.

"Vanilla as always," Madge asked, placing the milkshake in front of him and then continuing on with the rest of ours.

"A wonderful memory," The Magician said. "Now a glass of fine whiskey and a cigar and I would be as happy as can be."

"Drink your milkshake, Nick," Madge said, shaking her head and moving off to one side behind the booth. She never sat with us, but often took part in the meetings and it was clear she had no desire to miss this one.

"Good seeing you again, Stan," The Magician said, as he stirred his milkshake and sipped it.

I stared at Stan, then back at Nick Scipio, The Magician. Clearly they had history. And I was just about to ask what that history was when Lady Luck appeared and scooted into the booth beside her daughter.

"Nick," she said, nodding.

The Magician bowed slightly. "I am honored, as always."

"Cut the crap," Laverne said, "and explain to me what's happening and how you know about it."

When Lady Luck gets blunt, things really have to be going wrong. This just looked worse and worse by the moment.

Three

THE MAGICIAN DIDN'T let Lady Luck's brashness even seem to phase him. He took a sip of his milkshake, nodded a thank-you in Madge's direction, and then turned to face Lady Luck.

From my position beside Patty across from Teri and her mother, I could see Nick's dark eyes. And I watched them closely as he spoke, seeing if I could get a read on him and if he was lying.

"In my little confines," The Magician said, "which are very comfortable, I might add, I have sometimes been able to see out ahead in time. Not far, and often not that accurately, since the future is always in flux by events of the present. But I did see that in two days all the 13th floors of every building in Las Vegas will become invisible. For some reason, all authorities will, at the time, know this will happen and will have all the floors from twelve-up completely evacuated. It will cause a very large event that will be difficult at best to explain away, except as a magician's illusion gone horribly wrong."

"I know all that," Laverne said, waving her hand in dismissal. "So who could actually pull off this kind of illusion?"

"Besides me?" The Magician asked. "No one. Which is why I don't think this is an illusion."

"Magic?" Stan asked as Lady Luck frowned.

Silence fell over the booth. And I had no idea why so many of them were upset.

We were sitting in a booth in an invisible office five hundred feet above the MGM Grand Hotel and Casino. If that wasn't magic, what were we talking about?

"So who could pull off this level of magic?" Lady Luck finally asked. "And why would anyone break the ban?"

I wanted to scream WHAT BAN? But instead I just sat watching The Magician. From what I could tell, he had been telling the truth and seemed as worried as the rest of the people around the table.

I'm sure I looked worried as well, but not for the same reason. I was worried because I had no idea what they were talking about.

"I don't know the answer to that," The Magician said. "But I will be glad to help find out. If this actually happens, it will give all magicians a bad name and magicians in general will take the blame since it will be the only way to explain away such an event."

"Thanks," Lady Luck said, nodding. "You up for talking to your people?"

He took another long sip of the vanilla milkshake, then nodded. "Let's go."

"The rest of you keep working on this," Laverne said.

And she and The Magician vanished.

I sat there in the silence they left behind, so confused I didn't even have a question to ask. So Patty got the ball rolling.

"What did he do?"

Stan shook his head. "Not much, actually. Just pissed off the wrong god at the wrong time with a stupid trick. He and Laverne actually like each other, so she put him in a comfortable cell to keep him out of the way for a few centuries. He comes out, or as he likes to call it, "escapes" when he wants or needs to."

"So," I said, taking a deep breath, "someone want to explain to me the difference in magic and what is holding this office in the air?"

Screamer and Teri both laughed and Stan just shook his head. Patty just patted my leg, which meant my question was really stupid.

"Real magic," Teri said, "not the illusions that magicians do, is powered from the dark side. It does not come from any one person or skill, but by tapping into the pool of dark energy that rests just under the surface of everything."

Stan nodded and looked at me. "Your power to teleport, step between moments of time, and keep this place in the air comes from you, the depth of your ability to help others. It is a power of your mind and who you are. Just as studying another person and knowing how they are going to act in a hand of cards is a trained skill.

"Okay," was all I could manage to say. I sure didn't feel like I had a powerful mind. Far from it at the moment, in fact.

"That's why some of us can see slightly into the future as well," Stan said. "Like you watch a person and can predict a play or know his cards, others can watch life and know what might be possible in the future. A skill."

Well, that sort of explained that question at least, so I nodded.

He looked squarely at me and then went on, his tone and voice very, very clear. "All our powers are powers of light and come out of who we are and our own skills and talents. Nothing we do is actually magic."

I decided to just keep pushing my ignorance out there for everyone to see. "So this stunt of making entire floors invisible comes from a magic that is banned?"

Stan and Terri both nodded.

Stan said, "Actual magic has been banned for centuries, but some people try it anyway at times."

"And what happens to them?" Patty asked.

"The dark magic consumes them," Screamer said, his voice sounding disgusted. "And they became part of the dark pool of power. Not something I would ever want to experience. Think of the worst images of hell and multiply that by one hundred."

With that the silence just settled over the room again. Outside the windows, the sun was shining, planes were landing at the airport, and the world kept going, unaware that entire slices of buildings were about to vanish.

I took a sip of my milkshake and let the coolness calm me a little. I just couldn't get one word out of my head and I finally just blurted it out.

"Why?"

"Why do they get consumed?" Screamer asked, looking at me as if I had lost my mind completely.

"No," I said, shaking my head. "Why make floors invisible? If this really is someone using magic and risking his or her life to do so, why do this stunt? It seems very petty, has no obvious return for the stunt, and flat makes no sense."

And yet again the silence filled my office around the booth.

I was right.

I knew it.

And their lack of an answer confirmed that for me.

No one who knew how to do dark magic and the repercussions from the use of dark magic would ever do something this stupid and out in the open.

And for no gain that I could see.

Suddenly I had yet another idea.

"What happens if this isn't real dark magic? What happens if it is a superhero having some issues with power control?"

Stan looked at me with a look that I couldn't read, but that wasn't unusual for me with Stan. He was the God of Poker, after all.

"Are you suggesting," Screamer asked, leaning forward, "that what is about to happen to all the 13th floors might be nothing more than an accident about to happen?"

"Possible," I said. "So what kind of superhero needs to learn to make things vanish in their training?"

Teri started to say something, then shut her mouth and shook her head.

Screamer just shook his head.

Stan and Patty both said nothing.

Finally, from behind the booth Madge said, "Cleaners. And some food superheroes as well."

"Like you made our lunch remains vanish," I said, glancing back at her.

She nodded.

"Are there Gods of Cleaners and Superheroes of cleaning?" I asked, then knew the answer. Of course there were. I had watched a person come into a room and it seemed to just get clean, as if by some sort of magic, which was more-than-likely a special power. I always admired people who could do that type of cleaning, since every time I tried to clean something, it looked worse instead of better.

"Damn," Stan said softly. Then he said, "Everyone's with me."

"Except me," Madge said. "I'll have milkshakes ready for you when you get back."

Stan nodded and then a moment later all five of us were standing in a huge warehouse that smelled of ammonia and other cleaning solutions.

Four

THE BUILDING AROUND us was so large I couldn't see any wall in any direction. Nothing but aisles between huge stacks of cases of what looked like varied cleaning solutions and supplies.

The roof had to be ten stories overhead, the lights dim, the floor smooth concrete, and the temperature worse than air conditioning set too low. The stack closest to me had to go up four or five stories into the air, pallet on top of pallet. How they stayed stacked like that was anyone's guess, or how anyone did the stacking was another skill I really didn't want to watch anytime soon.

A moment after we arrived, the Magician and Lady Luck arrived as well.

She turned to me. "You think this might be a new superhero having issues with powers?"

I nodded. "An idea that makes sense. Other than to do as an illusion, this future event makes no sense otherwise."

The Magician nodded. "Now I see why these people hang around with you."

"Thanks," I said, "but why are we standing here in this warehouse?"

"What, you don't like my office or something?" a voice blurted behind me.

I spun around to face a short, stout, matronly woman wearing a light blue cleaning uniform. On the cloth sewn-on name badge it read "Hygieia" and under that it said in small letters "Call me Jean."

Laverne stepped up in front of me to face the new woman before I could say anything about her "office."

"Jean, thanks for meeting with us," Laverne said, her voice very stern, so much so that I shuddered slightly. "Every

13th floor of every building in Las Vegas is going to vanish in just under two days."

"Good," Jean said, shrugging. "We won't have to clean them."

"We think it's one of your people who is going to cause the problem," Laverne said.

She frowned at Laverne, started to say something, then stopped and really looked around at all of us. "Stan, Poker Boy, Patty Ledgerwood, Screamer, your daughter, and The Magician. You have the A-Team on this, so it must be serious."

"It is," Laverne said. "Very serious. We can't let this happen. Are you training someone in the Las Vegas area?"

"Always training someone it seems," Jean said.

Beside her a very, very short man appeared wearing a hood over his head and only allowing just part of his face to show. I had no idea who he was or what his job was.

"You are training one called Dee, my sister," the short man said, his voice very deep.

"Oh, yeah, her," Jean said, nodding. "She's a strange talent, very powerful, only been on the job a few months, but seems to learn quickly."

"She has many fears," the short man said. Then he vanished.

At that point I had about fifty questions I wanted to ask, but as I had learned years before, when dealing with Gods, it was better to just keep silent and let them go on and then have someone explain later what happened.

"I'm not sure how Dee having fears could cause this," Jean said, looking puzzled.

"Maybe she's afraid of the number thirteen," I said, instantly breaking my rule about keeping my mouth shut.

Silence.

And in a huge warehouse with the ceiling towering four stories over my head, that silence seemed awful loud as everyone stared at me.

Finally Jean said, "I will bring Dee."

I instantly felt sorry for the poor girl. If I had been brought into a group like this, I would have more than likely fainted during my first years of being a superhero.

"Hold on," I said before the God of Cleaning could jump away. "I'm afraid, as a new superhero, she won't be able to answer any questions with a crowd like this. This group still intimidates me at times and I've been at this for a decade or so."

Jean nodded. "What would you suggest, Poker Boy?"

"Patty and I could go talk with her alone and the rest of you can keep track of how the conversation goes."

Jean glanced at Laverne who nodded.

"She is working on the third floor of the Golden Nugget. Tall, skinny, very young and very smart."

"Blind camera spot end of the hall," Stan said, "against the wall across from the elevators."

I nodded and jumped with Patty to that spot.

Five

FAINT MUSIC PLAYED in the hallway and it smelled like the carpets had just been vacuumed. Down the plush hallway to our right was a maid's cart, so we headed in that direction.

As we neared the cart a tall woman with red hair appeared wearing a maid's uniform and carrying an armload of towels. She smiled at us, then dropped the towels into her cart. She was very young and hadn't yet seemed to grow into her body or her face.

It was clearly Dee. Under the sleeves of her shirt I could see signs of tattoos and another tattoo peaked out of her high collar.

As she started to turn back to go into the room I said, "Dee, we need to talk with you."

She stopped, suddenly looking puzzled. Her bright green eyes got very round.

"I am Poker Boy, this is Patty Ledgerwood."

Patty extended her hand. "Great to meet you," Patty said, giving the young superhero her best calming power.

Dee shook Patty's hand and seemed to relax a little. I didn't add in my calming power just yet, but I had a hunch I was going to need it.

"Your boss, Jean, says great things about you," I said.

Suddenly Dee looked panicked again. I remember early on in my superhero starting months, I thought no one knew I was secretly a superhero, so I was always shocked when another person knew that. Like me, she was going to be surprised as she learned just how many superheroes and gods there really were.

At the end of the hallway, the elevator dinged and the door started to open. So I slipped us out of time and into an instant between moments of time so that we wouldn't be disturbed. Since we were in a hallway and couldn't hear any traffic noise outside, nothing seemed to change, so Dee didn't notice.

"How do you know Jean?" Dee asked, looking first at Patty, who was still smiling and then back at me.

"We know many of the different gods," Patty said. "I work in the hospitality area and Poker Boy here works in the poker area, just as you work in the cleaning area. We are all at the same level, just under different departments."

Dee nodded and relaxed again. This girl really, really was the nervous type, of that there was no doubt.

I decided since Jean and Laverne and Stan were watching, to just jump to the problem. "Dee, are you scheduled in two days to clean Floor 14 here?"

Panic flipped across Dee's face and I sent calming waves at her, just as Patty was doing, trying to help her stay under control. I could feel my calming and trust-me power boosted a little as well, more than likely from Stan.

Dee calmed down and then nodded. "It's the 13th floor and I'm deathly afraid of it. I don't know what to do."

"We can help," Patty said, smiling as both of us kept aiming our combined calming powers at the young superhero. We were hitting Dee with so much calming juice, we could have put a horse to sleep smiling.

"But it's part of my job to clean that floor," Dee said, looking like she was about to burst into tears.

Suddenly I had another idea.

"We can help with that if you let us," I said. "We can help you never fear anything with the number 13 again."

"You could do that?" Dee asked. "And Jean wouldn't mind?"

"If it's going to help you do your job," Patty said, "I'm sure she wouldn't mind at all."

Dee stared at me, then at Patty for a moment. I could feel Stan boosting my "trust me" power I was pouring at Dee.

Finally Dee nodded.

"Stan, bring Screamer," I said into the air.

A moment later Stan and Screamer appeared.

Dee jumped. "Are you gods?"

"He is," Screamer said, smiling at Dee as he pointed at Stan. "Great to meet you, Dee."

Screamer extended his hand and the moment he touched Dee, she froze.

Patty and I kept our calming powers aimed at Dee and turned up to full power.

"Need help to clean this out, Stan," Screamer said.

Stan nodded and touched Screamer's shoulder. I knew at that moment in time they were both inside Dee's mind, working to clear out her fears of the number thirteen without really hurting her or changing her in any way and leaving no trace they had been in there.

After a moment Stan nodded and dropped his hand from Screamer's shoulder. Then Screamer let go of Dee's hand.

"So what can you do to help me?" Dee asked, staring at Screamer and then at Stan.

"Do you still fear the number thirteen?" I asked.

She frowned for a moment, then shook her head. "No, I don't. Wow, you guys are good."

"We'll let you get back to work now," Patty said, touching Dee's arm one more time to really leave a calming and pleasant feel with the young superhero.

"Thanks," Dee said, smiling. "I hope to see you again."

As I dropped the time shield and jumped all of us back to my office in the air over the MGM Grand Hotel, all I kept thinking about was that I had no doubt we

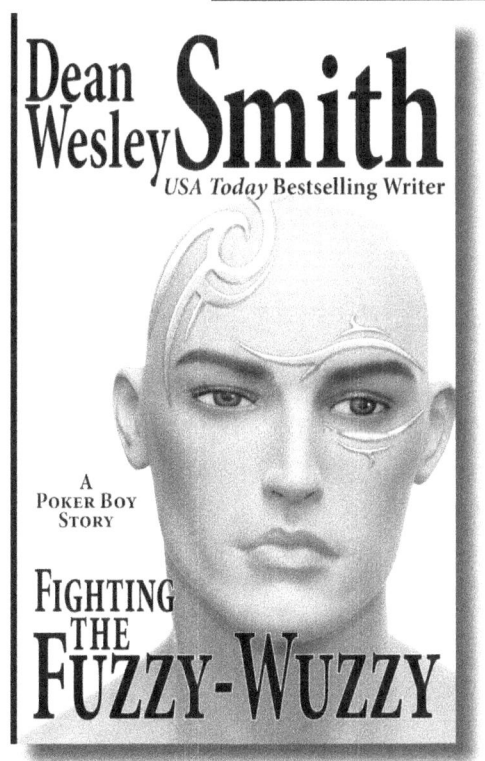

were going to see more of that young superhero in the future. I had a hunch she might just be helping the team down the road at times.

I guess that was my way of seeing into the future a little.

Madge was waiting for us with freshly made milkshakes. Laverne and The Magician and Terri appeared a moment after we did.

"Jean thanks you all," Laverne said. "As do I."

"I thank you as well," The Magician said, bowing slightly. "Your quick thinking and action has saved illusionists everywhere from a very difficult black eye."

Smiling, I slid into the booth and Patty slid in beside me as Terri gave Screamer a big kiss and then joined us.

It had seemed like hours ago that my French fries had disappeared from the table, but actually, this time, we had saved the city in just under a half hour.

"Madge," I asked, smiling at her as she placed the last milkshake on the table, "is there any chance you could make those French fries reappear?"

"Make that two orders," Lady Luck said, sliding into the booth beside her daughter.

"Three, if you don't mind," The Magician said, pulling up a chair.

Madge laughed and turned for the door to the Diner. "I had a hunch you would want some after lunch got shortened, so four orders of fries are cooking right now."

"Seeing the future again, Miss Madge?" The Magician asked, winking.

She smiled at him and winked back. "Depends if you have enough magic up that sleeve of yours to handle a future me."

"Have I ever failed you, Miss Madge?"

Madge laughed like a young girl and disappeared through the door.

All Patty and I and Screamer and Terri could do was just stare open-mouthed at The Magician as he sipped on his milkshake, smiling.

Lady Luck just shook her head as I tried desperately to clear the image out of my mind of a tall, skinny elf and an overweight waitress together.

I have a hunch it's burned there forever.

~

Year One (so far)

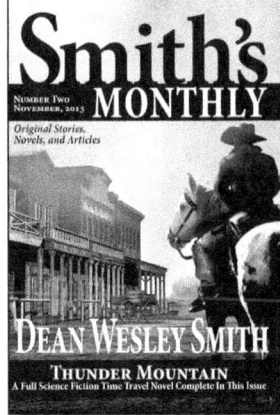

A subscription to *Smith's Monthly* saves you money and ensures you receive a monthly dose of diverse reading from *USA Today* bestselling author Dean Wesley Smith. Subscriptions are available in electronic and trade paper formats and begin with the very next volume. Subscribe today at www.SmithsMonthly.com. And if you missed one of these previously published issues, they're available from your favorite bookstore or online retailer.

DEAN WESLEY SMITH

THE ADVENTURES OF

HAWK

Chapters 22-25

What came before...

Nineteen-year-old Danny Hawk, his uncle, and his best friend Craig, were in Cairo to look for his missing father. Danny had witnessed the death of his only contact in Cairo, Professor Davis, because the professor had Danny's father's journals.

Danny knows that the men who had killed the professor were now after him and the journals. Danny finds the journals and gets his uncle and friend to safety in an airport hotel where he tells them what happened. They decide to keep searching for Danny's father and try to rescue him.

Along the way, Danny and Craig find some help from a street kid named Bud and twins from South Africa who had worked with Danny's father.

They managed to escape the men chasing them twice so far, Danny wasn't sure their luck would hold a third time.

And it barely did. They finally decided to head out of Cairo.

Beyond the headwaters of the Amazon, in the Republic of Congo, after a few more close calls, they hire a guide to take them into the jungle in search of a lost ancient city.

And even into the jungle on the Trail of Elephants, they are followed.

THE ADVENTURES OF HAWK

CHAPTER TWENTY-TWO

September 15, 1970
Deep in the jungle, Republic of Congo

HASSETT HAD CRAIG, the twins, and Bud hide in the jungle to the right of the path of elephants and warned them to not move for any reason, no matter what they heard or what happened. Then he used a branch to brush away their footprints where they had all entered the deep underbrush. Danny and Hassett also both left their packs, but Hassett kept a rifle he had been carrying over his shoulder.

"This way," Hassett said, turning and moving uphill through the jungle. Danny stayed with him for ten minutes, breathing hard and sweating even harder. Finally, Hassett held up his hand for Danny to be quiet, then moved to the edge of the jungle.

"Make no sudden movements," he whispered.

He then led Danny over a shallow rise along the edge of the jungle. It took a moment for Danny to realize what he was seeing. The half-mile-wide path had turned almost gray under the high trees ahead. Thousands and thousands of elephants were grazing and moving slowly down the hill.

"How did you know they were here?" Danny whispered.

Hassett pointed at the circling flocks of small birds. "They go where the elephants go."

The elephants smell was thick in the air, like baskets of apples that had been left in the sun for days.

Danny had never seen an African elephant, and was stunned at their size, and of the size of the tusks the bulls had. He had heard that ivory poaching had been bad in some areas, but it didn't look like this massive herd had been found yet.

Danny stayed close to Hassett, moving as silently as he could as they worked their way past the elephants, past the lead bull who stood guard.

Hassett moved the two of them slightly out into the path above the elephants, then handed Danny some dry brush. "Get ready to wave this and run at them," Hassett said.

Danny finally understood what Hassett was planning.

Hassett grabbed another handful of long, dry grass, then took his rifle off his shoulder.

He lit Danny's brush with a pocket lighter, then his own.

"Now!"

Waving the burning grass in his hand, Danny ran at the herd of huge beasts, shouting as loud as he could.

Hassett did the same, firing his rifle into the air at the same time.

The noise and the sight of the flames spooked the herd almost instantly.

The bull trumpeted a warning, as did others, and almost as one, the entire herd turned and started down the path at a full run.

For a moment, all Danny could see was a massive wall of elephant butts disappearing into a cloud of dust.

Thousands of huge animals, all weighing thousands of pounds, all running at the same time. It was a sight that Danny had never imagined, or thought of ever seeing.

Danny dropped his torch and stamped it out.

Hassett did the same.

A couple of bull elephants trumpeted so loudly that Danny bet it could be heard miles below on Lake Albert.

The elephant stampede shook the ground like a strong earthquake, and the rumbling echoed over the jungle. The huge dust cloud drifted out over the jungle.

"How far will they run?" Danny shouted to Hassett over the intense noise.

"Far enough to take care of our friends and cover our tracks!" Hassett shouted back.

They stood and watched the amazing sight for a few moments, then Hassett led Danny back to the edge of the jungle. They plowed into the underbrush, staying in the deep jungle as they moved back down the hill toward Craig and the others.

He and Hassett joined up with Craig and the others, and with Hassett indicating they should be very quiet, he turned and led them deeper into the jungle, away from the path of elephants.

A very long, hot hour later of fighting their way down what seemed to be a narrow animal path, Danny finally asked Hassett, "When are we going to get to the lost city?"

Hassett laughed and kept going. "You've been in it for fifteen minutes."

That got all of them looking around, and now that Hassett had said that, Danny could see odd shapes buried by the dense growth of the jungle.

"How big was this place?" Craig asked, shouting his question over Danny's shoulder to Hassett.

Hassett entered a small meadow and stopped, dropping his pack in the shade under some large trees. "I figure that over a half million people lived here six or seven thousand years ago."

"Half million?" Danny said softly. He couldn't even imagine that, standing here in the jungle now. It would be like standing in downtown Los Angeles, after it was overgrown and all the tall buildings knocked down, and trying to imagine the size of the city.

"Welcome to the city of Ishango," Hassett said, waving his arm around in a wide circle.

He moved about twenty steps to one side of the meadow, beside what looked like a wall of vegetation and yanked on some growth, pulling aside the green to show stone blocks underneath.

Danny followed the angle of the green wall up through the trees, stunned as his mind tried to grasp what he was seeing.

"It's a temple," Ed said, his voice hushed.

"It seems we found our teaming masses," Craig said, shaking his head and looking around.

"Teaming masses?" Dr. Hassett asked.

Danny nodded. "Under the teaming masses, the river becomes clear, the path muddy."

"The third Hydra Journal entry?" Dr. Hassett asked.

Danny nodded. "It would seem that the teaming masses were the half million people who lived here."

"Well, I'll be," Hassett said, shaking his head and laughing. "I was so busy looking up, I never thought in twenty years to look down. I have no idea what's under this ancient city."

Danny had no doubt that to continue the search for his father, they needed to find out.

CHAPTER TWENTY-THREE

September 17, 1970
Lost City of Ishango, Deep in the jungle of the Republic of Congo.

TWO LONG DAYS of searching later, Danny finally had some luck, but not the kind he had hoped for. The ground dropped away under him like an elevator suddenly falling.

Danny, with his best friend, Craig James, had been exploring the ground floor on an ancient temple in the lost city of Ishango. The city, at one point, had been the home of over a million people, long before the Pharaohs ruled in Egypt. Now, Danny and the others were looking for any passage that would lead them under the ruins of the old city covered in jungle.

Danny had been using a burning torch for light to explore a dark room in the back of the old temple while Craig went on down a narrow hallway.

The thousands of years of jungle and hot weather had left nothing of the old city except the stones with which the Ishango people had built the city. If there had ever been wooden doors, they were long gone. And every stone structure was completely covered by jungle and shaded by tall trees. In the dark rooms inside the stone buildings, nothing lived except small animals and insects.

In two days, Danny had seen more large spiders than in a bad horror movie. So far, all of them had avoided the huge creatures hovering in webs in the dark rooms. The last thing any of them needed thousands of miles from any civilization and good doctors was to be bitten by a poisonous spider.

Or any other jungle creature for that matter.

As the floor dropped out from under him with a loud crack and Danny fell, he did two things, almost instinctively, and at the same time.

First, he shouted. "Craig!"

Second, as what he thought was a solid rock floor dropped away into blackness, he twisted around like a drill the coach had made them do in football practice last year.

That way he was facing what he thought was the outside wall of the building.

He found himself falling through an open space filled with twisted roots.

He frantically grabbed for anything to slow his fall.

Everything went into slow motion as he grabbed and ripped out handfuls of thin roots.

Finally, one of the roots held, but his grip didn't, and his momentum yanked his hand off the root as it swung him around.

But it slowed him enough to grab more roots, and they held.

After a moment, he found himself swinging in midair, close to what looked like a tall stone wall, holding on with all his might to handfuls of tree and plant roots.

His hands and shoulders hurt, but he was still alive.

Around him was complete darkness.

He couldn't even see his arms going past his face.

The air was cool and smelled of damp earth and mold.

There was a faint, distant sound of water running.

He forced himself to remain as still as he could and take deep breaths to let his pounding heart slow and his eyes adjust.

It became clear that he wasn't in complete darkness, but close.

Carefully, he then looked down.

His torch had fallen all the way through the roots and somehow remained lit, showing faint outlines of the huge cavern-like room. He could see that he still had a good fifty feet to drop from where he was hanging.

His breath caught. Oh, wow, luckily, the roots had been here, like a false ceiling on the huge underground area, otherwise he would have been very dead on those rocks below.

Above him, the hole into the room he had been in was an impossible twenty feet over his head. And there was nothing to climb on. The layer of roots didn't extend all the way to the hole.

And besides that, he didn't trust himself to let go of the roots he was holding.

He forced himself to take yet another deep breath. His hands and shoulders were aching. He couldn't hold himself here for very long.

He twisted carefully around and searched for any kind of ledge on the rock wall near where he hung.

At first, he couldn't see anything, but then he spotted a crack between two stones where more roots were growing out into the open area just below him. The crack didn't look to be more than a few inches wide, but it was more than he had now, if he could get to it.

He got swinging gently, almost holding his breath for fear he would break or pull out the roots holding him.

Finally, he managed to get one foot on the ledge. It was more than a crack. It was actually a thin ledge about an inch wide.

He eased around and pressed his back against the cold wall, using the heels of his shoes to take the pressure off his arms.

The ledge felt solid under his feet, but after falling through the floor of that room, he wasn't trusting anything at this point. He still kept his tight grip on the roots that had saved him. But at least they weren't holding his entire weight.

"Danny!"

Craig's voice echoed down to him from what seemed like an impossible distance away.

"Down here!" Danny shouted back. "But be careful. It's a long fall!"

The dark around him seemed to swallow Danny's voice. And it felt like something scampered across his feet on the ledge, but he ignored that. He didn't dare try to bend over. If he did, he would swing back out into space holding on to only the roots.

And he wasn't sure if he wanted to know what it was that lived in this dark cavern.

Above him, the light from Craig's torch outlined the hole where the rock floor Danny had been standing on had slipped away. Then Craig poked his head over the edge.

"Danny!" Craig shouted. Danny had no doubt that all Craig could see was his torch seventy feet below him on the rocks.

"About twenty feet below you," Danny said. "Stuck like Spider-Man on the wall."

"Oh, man, are you all right?" Craig asked, finally seeing Danny. "And how did you get there?"

"Just luck," Danny said. "But I think I found how to get under the old city."

"Yeah, I'd say," Craig said. "Can you hang on there? "I'll go get the others and some rope. Actually, a lot of rope."

"I'm not going anywhere," Danny said. "But hurry, would you?"

"Right back," Craig said.

His face and light disappeared from the hole over Danny's head.

He kept staring upward at the blackness, trying to let the training he had from his Native American grandfather take over and control his breathing.

Right now, more than anything, he needed to just remain still and calm.

Standing on the narrow ledge fifty feet over rocks, holding on to roots for dear life, there was just nothing else he could do.

Then, he felt something again move across his foot in the pitch darkness of the jungle cavern.

It felt very real and had weight.

Then the horrible thing started up his leg.

CHAPTER TWENTY-FOUR

September 17, 1970
Under the Lost City of Ishango, deep in the jungle of the Republic of Congo.

DANNY PRESSED HIS back against the stone wall. He took a slow, shallow breath to try to stop himself from screaming and panicking. On a thin ledge, with only a bunch of roots holding him in place, he didn't dare panic. That would be the quickest way to get himself killed, no matter what was crawling up his leg.

Slowly, using his left hand to hold onto all the roots that had saved his life, he pressed his back against the rock wall then took a swipe at the creature as it came above his knee in the dark.

The back of his hand hit something fairly solid and covered in some sort of fur. It felt huge, but Danny figured it was about the size of his fist. More than likely one of the big spiders.

Whatever it was went flying off into the darkness. He just hoped it went far enough that it wasn't coming back.

He sure didn't need to be fighting a mad spider in the dark while clinging to the face of a cliff.

He took a deep breath and forced himself to try to calm his racing heart and try to listen.

Nothing seemed to be moving around him.

Only the distant sound of running water broke the intense silence.

Under the teeming masses, the river becomes clear, the path muddy.

That was the third Hydra Journal entry Danny's father had found in Cairo.

It was the riddle that had led them here, to this ancient lost city. The half million people who lived here when the Hydra Journal was written were the teeming masses. And now Danny could hear the river, or at least it sounded like a river.

He had no idea what "the path muddy" meant, but he had a hunch, as with anything in this adventure so far, it wasn't going to be easy to figure out.

And even here in the dark, pressed against a cliff face, he half expected the men from the Hydra League to show up. The League had seemed to be able to track them just about anywhere they went. Their only hope, Danny figured, was that the elephants had taken care of them. Otherwise, they would show up here soon, if they weren't already here somewhere, just watching them.

The Hydra League had been formed when this city was still alive and had a half million people in it. They clearly knew these ruins were here. They were the ones protecting the secret of the Fountain of Youth.

And they were the ones who had kidnapped Danny's father.

Danny figured the only way of ever seeing his father again was to stay alive long enough to find and solve all ten of the Hydra Journal clues. A tall order for a guy stuck in the dark on a cliff.

"Danny!" Craig shouted from above. "Hang on, we're coming!"

Danny glanced up as a number of torches lit up the hole above him.

"Careful on that floor," Danny shouted up to his friends. "More sections of it might give way."

"You found the way under the city I see," Hassett said as he poked his head over the edge and looked down.

"I think it found me," Danny said. "And I hear running water."

Hassett laughed. "Perfect. Hang on, we're hooking up enough rope to get you all the way to the ground."

"Not going anywhere," Danny said, trying to adjust his grip on the roots that he had been holding onto with a death grip for what seemed like an eternity now.

Hassett, the old guide they had hired to take them up the Trail of Elephants, had turned out to be Dr. Steven Hassett, world known archeologist who had been discredited for his belief that a major civ-

ilization had existed around the planet before the Pharaohs. He had been exploring and documenting the ancient city of Ishango for twenty years. And he knew Danny's father, and about the Hydra League and the Hydra Journals.

Danny was really glad to have him helping them.

A moment later a rope started down toward Danny. Craig stuck his head over the edge and watched it.

"That's enough," Craig said as the rope with a few knots in it got to Danny's level. It looked to be a thick rope, clearly something Hassett had in his camp hidden in the center of the old city.

"How far down do you think it is from there?" Hassett called out.

"Fifty feet, maybe sixty!" Danny shouted back up, glancing down at his flickering torch on the rocks below.

"Hang on," Craig said.

Danny watched as he looked around, then leaned back over the edge. "Okay, we're ready. You want a ride down?"

"I would love one," Danny said.

Craig took the rope and got it swinging slightly until finally the end got close enough for Danny to reach with one hand.

"Are you ready?" Danny shouted back up. "It's going to have to hold all my weight."

Craig glanced back over his shoulder, then shouted down, "Ready."

"Here goes," Danny said.

Letting go of the roots, he grabbed the rope right above one of the knots tied in it and swung out into space, twisting in the hundreds of roots that filled the space. He wrapped his legs around the rope, like he had done in gym class in Junior High.

He was living a childhood dream. He was in a jungle playing Tarzan, only he was underground, fifty feet above rocks, in the dark, with huge spiders, and scared to death.

Tarzan had it good.

The rope held and Danny swung through the maze of roots, breaking many of them, and wrapping others around his body. He used his arms to keep the roots away from his neck. The last thing he needed was to slip and have a root hang him.

He used his legs to support most of his weight on the rope, then with one hand he pulled off many of the roots before shouting, "Lower away!"

Less than five minutes later, he was on the rough rock surface of the cavern's floor.

He hadn't felt anything so good as solid ground under his feet. He hadn't realized until he was down just how frightened he had been. Now his hands started to shake.

"I'm down!" he shouted up to a tiny hole of light at least seven stories over his head.

All the way up, the rope had knots tied every five feet to make it easier to hold and climb. That was going to be a nasty climb to get back out of here.

"Tie the rope around a rock or anchor it in some way," Hassatt shouted down, his voice echoing in the large, dark cavern.

Danny did as Hassatt said, then shouted that it was secure.

"Coming down," Hassatt shouted.

The old archeologist had a large pack on his back and he came down the rope like a monkey, faster than Danny could have done it. For a man in his sixties, Hassatt was in great shape, that was for sure.

He got to the bottom and then worked on starting another few torches.

The twins followed next, dropping quickly hand-over-hand, clearly also used to climbing ropes. They both had packs of equipment as well. Bud came down next, with a bag of something in his mouth. He was slower, clearly more afraid of the height than of climbing down the rope. Craig was last and the slowest, not taking any chances.

Craig patted Danny on the shoulder after they were all standing on the rough floor of the cavern. "Glad you're all right."

"Thank all the roots," Danny said.

"Well, at least we found this," Hassatt said, holding his torch up and studying the huge cavern around them. "The original residents clearly used these caverns."

He pointed to some old stone stairs leading down toward a lower cavern in the direction of the water, now clear in the light of six burning torches. The smoke from the torches twisted upward into the dark of the maze of roots.

Danny finally took time to really look around at the cavern he'd found.

Some of the walls were stone blocks as well. And part of the ceiling was the stone floor of the temple above them. A lot of rock had fallen in places, and the hole over their head seemed to be the only way out. The temple had been built over this cavern for a reason, of that there was no doubt. Now they just had to find the reason.

"Well," Craig said, shaking his head. "At least those Hydra League thugs won't find us down here."

"I wouldn't count on it," a distant voice said from over their heads.

All of their heads snapped to look up as if tied to the same string. There was a faint light in the hole above, and a few shadows moving around.

Danny knew that voice. It was the same man who had killed the professor back in Cairo.

How could they have found them?

Clearly they had escaped the elephants and had just been watching them the last few days.

As all six of them stared upward, the rope fell toward them, forming a huge pile with a thump at their feet.

The end had clearly been cut.

Now they had no way out.

"Enjoy your stay," the voice above them said.

Then he laughed, the sound echoing in the huge chamber like a bad villain in a bad movie.

Only this was real.

Very real.

Continued in the next issue…

USA *Today* Bestselling Writer

DEAN WESLEY SMITH

*She Loved the Sex,
But She Loved
the Killing More...*

A PATHETIC FALLACY

USA Today *bestselling writer, Dean Wesley Smith, takes a look at a very strange job that Connie works. She loves the sex, but she loves the killing more.*

The job certainly keeps her life exciting in more ways than she can imagine.

A story that walks a very thin line between an adult fantasy and The Twilight Zone.

A PATHETIC FALLACY

Harold: The First Trick.

CONNIE ROLLED SIDEWAYS on the bed. The hot, sticky air of the small New York City hotel room made the sheets seem damp from more than just the sweat of their bodies. Outside she could faintly hear the sounds of the city, the honking of the cars, the rumble of the subways, the constant hum of millions of busy people. The sounds made her feel safe, sure of herself. They always had, even as a kid.

She propped herself up on her elbow and let herself enjoy the smell of new sex mixed with Harold's cologne and his slightly sour body odor. He had his face buried in the pillow and his breathing was heavy and hard.

"You going to be all right?" she asked, rubbing his back and shoulders lightly, letting the sweat roll under her fingers, his smooth skin slick and hot. He had a great body even though he was almost fifty. He must exercise a lot.

He nodded, but didn't say a word.

She stretched, sat up cross-legged on the bed.

"That sure was nice," she said. They had made love for over an hour and she had lost count of her orgasms.

Again all he did was nod.

She smiled. She loved it when a man was totally satisfied, exhausted, and drained of energy.

Harold, she knew, worked for a brokerage firm. He had a wife and two kids. Both kids were in high school and he was worried about paying for their college. He owned a small summer place out on Long Island, but while in the city he had a flat near Central Park.

She patted his naked, white rump and leaned toward the nightstand. With a quick snap of the wrist she opened the drawer and pulled out a small revolver. Earlier, while Harold was in the bathroom, she had loaded it and made sure the safety was off.

Smiling, she placed the gun right against the back of Harold's neck, the barrel pointing up into his brain. With her other hand she slowly stroked his back.

He sighed.

"Feels good, doesn't it?"

She moved the gun just far enough away from his head so that when he nodded, his face still buried in the pillow, he wouldn't feel the gun.

Slowly, with her free hand, she pulled another pillow up and draped it over the gun to muffle the sound of the shot and keep the blood from spattering too much. She was planning on taking a shower anyhow, but it was easier if there was less blood.

"It was nice, Harold," she said and pulled the trigger.

The shot was no louder than she had expected. She doubted that someone passing by in the hall could have even heard it.

Harold flinched once, lay still.

She pulled the pillow off and looked at the mess she had made. Blood was soaking into the white of the pillow under

his head and there was a small round hole bleeding just above the line of his hair. She had no desire to see what the bullet leaving his head had done to his face. He had had a handsome face and she wanted to remember him that way.

The smell in the room had changed from sex and sweat to a copper smell of fresh blood. God how she loved that smell, almost more than anything else.

Even the sex.

She scooted away from Harold and off the bed.

Carefully, she laid the gun on the end table beside the bed and stretched, her back to the bed.

The window was open, with only the light, white drapes pulled for privacy. She moved to the window and was almost tempted to walk out nude onto the small balcony. But doing that in the middle of the day might draw just a little too much attention and that she didn't need at the moment.

So instead, she took comfort in just pulling back the drapes, sliding open the glass door slightly and breathing in the fresh, hot air and the smells of the city.

She stood there for a time, enjoying the feel of another job well done, and some good sex.

"Well, better get showered and dressed," she finally said and turned back from the window.

Harold was gone.

"What—?"

The bed was made, no blood anywhere.

"What the hell?"

She scrambled to the obviously freshly made bed and pulled the covers aside.

Nothing.

No body, no blood.

Nothing.

She looked under the bed and then quickly checked the closet and the bathroom.

Nothing.

Absolutely nothing except a fresh hotel room. And the main door to the room was still locked and bolted from the inside.

She dropped down into the armchair facing the dark television and stared at the room, not believing what she was seeing.

Not possible, just not possible.

"Get a grip on yourself, old girl," she said aloud. Her voice sounded hollow and almost ready to crack, even to her ears. "There has to be an explanation for this. Somehow?"

She forced herself to think about what had happened. She had been hired in her usual manner to kill Harold Lindsey. She had got him up here, made love to him, and then done exactly that.

She had killed him.

One shot. Nice and clean the way she liked.

Just as she had done to men before him.

He was nothing special.

She went back over the events following his shooting. She had placed the gun on the end table.

She got up and went over to the end table and checked the drawer. There was nothing there but a bible and some information about restaurants.

She had gone to the window next, so she repeated her steps and looked out the white drapes like she had the last time.

Everything out there seemed to be the same, including the sounds of the city.

She turned around, afraid for what she might find.

Harold's body was still gone.

The bed was still made.

She was still nude.

But this time the bathroom door was closed and she was sure she had left it open.

Her heart racing, she eased closer to the door and could hear movement in there.

She was about to grab her clothes and duck for the hall when the bathroom door opened and out stepped Harold, also totally nude.

And very much alive.

She took a step back, not really wanting to believe what she was seeing.

He also stopped and the look of shock on his face matched what she was feeling.

Finally, after what seemed like an eternity he said, "Connie. What—? I mean, how? I mean—"

He stopped and just stared at her.

She glanced at the door to the hall and tried to figure if she could make it with a quick dash. He was much closer and much bigger and stronger. Even with her training it would be a close match if it came down to a fight.

After another long moment of staring at each other, Harold seemed to recover a little. He made a quick step sideways, yanked open the top drawer of the cabinet under the television and pulled out a revolver.

"Look," he said. "I don't know what's going on here. You must be Connie's twin sister or something. And I don't know how you got in here, but I don't like it."

At the sight of the gun, she cursed herself silently for being so careless. Maybe she had been dreaming about killing Harold.

Or something. Maybe a daydream, planning how she would do it.

There had to be an explanation, and she bet anything he had it.

"My name is Connie, I don't have a twin, and you think I like being here any better than you do?"

She was bluffing, but she didn't know what else to do. She stood her ground, not even bothering to cover herself.

He laughed. "I don't believe you're Connie for a moment, although you do look like her a great deal. But I happen to know for a fact that Connie is dead."

This time it was her turn to laugh. "Actually, you're the one who is dead. That gun, one shot through the back of the head."

He smiled. "Oh, really?" He pointed the gun at her. "I don't think so. You see, your husband hired me to kill you."

She heard the crack of the gun and the impact of the bullet spun her around and she dropped back onto the made bed.

The last thing she remembered was the friendly sounds of the city going about its business.

Harold: The Sixteenth Trick

SHE HAD WATCHED him for days. He worked in a moderate-sized office building off Wall Street. He had four different suits he liked to wear, two gray, one brown, and one deep blue. His ties were always bright, but not too much.

At one every afternoon he went out to lunch, usually to a small deli two blocks up. He had a regular spot at the deli and normally ate alone, reading the paper or a magazine. He was never anywhere to be seen on weekends, leaving the city on the train for Long Island and returning before work on Monday morning.

He seemed to have no regular friends or a steady girlfriend or boyfriend. This was going to be one of her easier kills.

On Tuesday, she managed to be sitting at the table next to his at the deli when he came in. The deli was a traditional New York deli, long and fairly narrow, with a big white glass counter full of meats and breads along one side and shelves lining the other walls.

The place usually smelled of sausage and garlic, with a faint odor of fresh-baked bread. There were maybe fifteen tables scattered the length of the place, with four bunched up in the back.

She made sure she was facing the front, glanced up as he approached and caught his eye. Then she smiled and he nodded hello and sat down. It was a little forward for most New Yorkers, but not so much as he would notice, considering they were sitting so close in such a small place. She left before he did, happy at the start she had made.

He went somewhere else for lunch the next day, but on Thursday he was back and again she smiled at him. And this time she said hello before pretending to go back to reading her magazine.

He returned her smile and hello and she noticed that a few times during lunch he glanced over at her.

Again she left before he did, acting as if she was slightly late, and making sure she didn't glance in his direction. But she knew the bait was in the water and the hook was in his mouth. Now it was just a matter of time.

The next day she brought along one of the current best selling novels and when she smiled and said hello as he approached he asked if the book was good. She said so far she thought it was and as soon as she finished it she would let him know. He smiled at that and they spoke briefly twice more during lunch and then she made a point of saying good-bye before she left.

By Wednesday, he had joined her for lunch and on Friday afternoon they ended up at the Crown Hotel on the seventieth floor. For her the sex was good, but as soon as they finished he rolled off the bed and went into the bathroom before she had a chance to even get her gun out of the nightstand. So she laid sprawled out on the bed, pretending to sleep, waiting for him to return.

After a minute, the toilet flushed and he came out carrying a pistol.

Her gun.

And he had it pointed at her.

"Sorry, Connie."

"What are you doing?" she demanded as she sat up on the bed and faced him.

"Just doing what your husband hired me to do."

"My husband?"

Harold laughed. "How stupid did you think I was? Did you really think that pick-up at lunch would work? On the second day I followed you home. After the third lunch I found out your name and your husband's name." Harold laughed again. "Did you know he's a very jealous man?"

She knew her mouth was open as she listened to what he was saying. She wasn't married. She lived off 45th Street and worked freelance, doing any odd job she was hired to do that paid a great deal of money. Usually it was luring some horny man into a room and killing him. This guy was totally crazy and she was about to tell him so when he shrugged.

"It was nice," he said. "The sex, I mean." He indicated the messed sheets she was sitting on. "But now it's time to get on with it."

"No! Wait!" She held up her hand to get him to stop.

But the gun was already aimed at her.

The explosion was loud, much louder than she had expected.

The force of the impact spun her around and off the edge of the bed. The last faint thought she had was of surprise.

This just couldn't be happening.

Harold: The Twenty-second Trick.

SHE WAS RIDING him like a cowboy rides a bucking bronco, astride his hips as they thrust hard into the air. She had one hand on the wall above the bed and the other behind her on his thigh.

"Whoa there, big guy," she said, leaning forward and kissing his sweating forehead. "Let's go slow for a moment."

He smiled and kissed her back, then she sat up straight again, the pace almost relaxed.

She had been planning on killing him after they finished, just as she had done with over twenty others. But maybe she should try a little something different this time. Maybe she should do him while they're having sex. Kinky, but it might be interesting.

She rubbed his chest and then kissed him again. "Harold, you want to do me a favor?"

He smiled and kissed her back. "Anything?"

"Just close your eyes and let me ride you for a minute."

"Without moving?"

"Without moving," she said.

"I'm all yours," he said, relaxing into the bed and shutting his eyes.

Amazing how he trusted her completely, especially the first time like this.

She moved her hips slowly in a circular motion and leaned back and pulled open the drawer of the small end table next to the bed. Inside was her gun, loaded and ready.

She moved a little bit more and he moaned, opening his mouth a little.

She moved a little faster and he moaned even more, tilting his head back at just the right angle that she could point the gun between his teeth and at the roof of his mouth.

With one more good thrust she pulled the trigger.

Blood splattered over her and over a large part of the room as the pistol blew the top of his head off.

He jerked upwards and than lay quiet, amazingly still hard inside her.

"She patted his blood-splattered chest for a minute and then pulled off of him. In a smooth motion and without a look back she rolled off the bed and headed for the bathroom. What she needed now was a shower.

For the first minute the water going down the drain was pink from the blood, but she had done this before. Harold was not the first and he wouldn't be the last. This was her job and she did it. If she enjoyed it at the same time, so much the better.

She finished the shower and then took her time drying her hair before she came back out of the bathroom.

When she opened the door, Harold was sitting dressed on the made bed, her gun pointed at her.

"What—"

"Sorry I'm not going to get to partake in our little love-making session, but you see, I think that would be just a little too weird."

"Weird?" she asked.

She glanced quickly around the room. No sign of all the blood. And the room smelled fresh.

This couldn't be happening.

She had just killed him.

"Why," he said, "to make love to you and then kill you. Guess I'm just not that weird, so I've decided to just kill you." He looked up and down her naked body. "But I see that might have been a mistake. Oh, well."

He raised the gun.

She put up her hand to stop him, but the explosion sent her spinning back onto the white tiles of the bathroom floor. Her last thoughts were of watching her own blood smear across the smooth, cold surface.

Harold: The Thirty-first Trick

SHE STOOD WITH her arm linked through his at the desk of the Crown Hotel as they registered. It had been a great two weeks tracking him until she finally got him talking in the deli. He was going to be one of her best kills. She'd have to do it in a special way for him, especially if he was good in bed.

Harold was filling out the check-in form when the clerk asked, "Did you folks have a good summer? We missed you around here."

Harold did what he could. He leaned forward and whispered "Hush, man. She doesn't know I'm married."

The clerk looked shocked for a moment, then remembered and looked embarrassed. He glanced at her and she winked at him, but the mood was spoiled. It just wasn't going to work this time.

And after such a good start, too.

But Harold gave it his best, even though he knew the clerk had messed it up.

After they made uninspired love, boring love like they used to do before the murders, he raised up on his elbow and looked at her. "You think we should go to a new hotel next time?"

She shook her head no. "They've treated us well for years. It was just a slip." She didn't say that she couldn't go back to those boring nights with him. No matter how much she loved him, they had to do something to spice things up to keep the marriage alive.

He nodded, looking thoughtful.

She rolled off the bed and went to the window.

Outside the sounds of the city covered the quiet of the room. For some reason the massiveness of those sounds soothed her, brought her back to reality, to what she was hired to do.

She must kill Harold.

She silently thanked the city for the help and turned back to face him.

But the room was empty, the bed made, and her clothes stacked neatly on the armchair.

On top of the pile was her gun, waiting.

She walked over and picked up the gun, the cold heaviness of it in her hand reassuring.

She checked it over, making sure it was fully loaded.

Then she smiled.

Harold always did know what would make her happy.

~

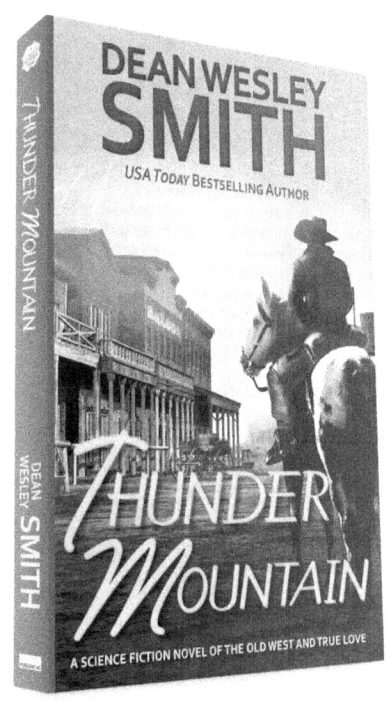

FICTION RIVER: YEAR ONE

Missed a volume from Fiction River's first year?

No problem. Buy individual volumes anytime from your favorite bookseller.

See why *Adventures Fantastic* calls *Fiction River* "one of the best and most exciting publications in the field today."

FICTION RIVER: YEAR TWO

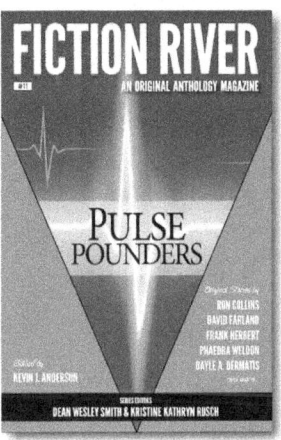

USA *Today* Bestselling Writer

DEAN WESLEY SMITH

THE MOUTH THAT WALKED

Cats seem to not care much about anything around them. Anyone who knows cats knows this to be not true. And watching a cat stalk and kill a mouse or bird shows yet another side of the creatures we let live with us.

This story, originally published in Amazing Stories *back in the late 1980s warns those who don't know cats what they can do when pushed. A cautionary tale.*

At times, because of the nature of older stories appearing and vanishing in moments, I will use this magazine to spotlight a favorite story of mine from the past. For this story, Amazing Stories *was on the verge of folding in that incarnation when I sold it to them, so very few people saw the story at publication, and no one under forty would have had a chance to ever read it. So I'm jumping the story forward in time. Enjoy.*

THE MOUTH THAT WALKED

One

CRAIG LIEBERMAN SUCKED at the two inch long scratch on the back of his hand and developed his new rule: Never pet a cat.

Never.

Not on the street.

Not on the steps to his building.

Not even if one brushed up against his leg outside his apartment door. He would never again stop to pet a cat.

Damn things were obnoxious, anyhow. Half the time they smelled of wet fur or rotted fish. They never came when a person called and the only half-good thing they did was kill rats.

He sucked on the scratch even harder, pulling the faint taste of blood into his mouth. The scratch would probably get infected. There was no telling where that cat's claw had been.

He looked back down the street at the yellow tom and resisted an impulse to pick up a rock. Damn thing. It had ruined any chance of friendship with any other cat. Craig Lieberman never forgot and he wouldn't forget his new rule.

At the next corner, he turned toward his apartment instead of going toward the library. He'd better get home and get some disinfectant on the scratch before it ended up costing him a trip to the doctor. His usual reading of the daily paper could wait.

Important things first.

In the next two blocks he saw seven cats.

The first three he avoided, the next two he kicked at and missed, and the other two he threw rocks at.

The last marble-sized rock hit a small black and white cat just above the right front leg and sent it running up an alley. The direct hit gave Craig a small thrill deep in his stomach. That would show those damn cats that they couldn't get away with scratching just anyone who showed a little kindness.

Stupid animals, anyhow.

Half a block later, he rounded the corner onto his street and stopped cold. The front steps of his apartment building were covered with cats. There had to be a hundred of them, their fur a rainbow of colors.

Craig hadn't seen that many cats in one place since he had visited an animal shelter when he was a child.

Craig started to move toward them.

In unison, they turned and looked at him.

The light film of warm sweat that covered his face turned ice cold, as if someone had slammed him straight from the warm summer day into a deep freeze.

He could feel their stares like needles jabbing his skin. The weight of their aloofness held him tight. He suddenly knew, without a doubt, exactly how little he mattered to them.

He was nothing.

It was below them to even acknowledge that he existed.

But they did, in unison, and then, as if on signal, they all looked away.

The sudden fear and crystal clear awareness that he had felt melted like a sliver of ice dropped on hot pavement. His first impulse was to turn and run for the police station, but the little voice in his head told him he was just being stupid. Besides, it would do no good. The cats would simply be gone by the time he got back and then the police would laugh.

He laughed at himself instead. What harm could cats do him?

None. They were just cats.

The heat of the day must have gotten to him. That's what had happened.

He was just about to pull out his handkerchief and dry his forehead when he noticed a man in a gray suit sitting in the middle of the cats. Craig would have sworn the man hadn't been there a few moments before. He hadn't been.

Craig was sure.

The steps had been covered only with cats. The man had somehow come up out of the middle of them. Craig shook his head at that thought.

Sunstroke.

He'd better get inside quick.

The man motioned for Craig to come closer.

Craig studied the cats and the man, then took a deep breath and moved forward. His own hallucination couldn't bother him. He'd get inside, call the doctor, and then lie down. He'd be fine in an hour or two.

Not one of the cats looked at him.

Craig hesitated, then stopped just short of the bottom step. The cats weren't going away.

"We need to talk," the man in gray said.

The man's voice was deep, his words clear, yet somehow flowing together. Craig studied the deep lines in the man's face. The man was both old, yet somehow very young. And his eyes bothered Craig. Cat eyes: Large and green, with bright yellow flakes of color, like gold scattered through solid rock.

"These your cats?" Craig asked after a moment, avoiding the man's gaze and making a sweeping motion with his arm at the steps. "You really can't have them here. I could call the Super and—"

The man laughed softly and the cats around him stirred without looking up at Craig. "No one truly owns a cat. All good people know that. We came to talk to you."

"Look, I'd like to get into my building. I don't think I'm feeling well. So, if you don't mind, could you have a few of your friends move aside and…"

"We need to talk," the man said softly, but firmly.

Craig realized he wasn't going to get anywhere by pushing. And no way was he going to go wading up into those cats. They'd rip the cuffs of his pants to shreds and he'd only had this pair for a few years. Besides, he'd already been hurt today.

"So go ahead and talk," Craig said.

"We would first like to apologize for the cut on your hand. As with most scratches, it was an accident."

Craig looked quickly down at the red scratch on the back of his hand. "How'd you know about that? And just who are you apologizing for?"

"I talk for myself and for those you call cats," he said softly. "It is my curse. I am known as The Mouth That Walks. It

> **No one truly owns a cat. All good people know that.**

is my plight to deal with humans on their own level. Would you accept our apology for the scratch?"

Craig scanned the cats. They didn't look at him. None of the other passersby on the street seemed to even notice anything was strange. This was just too much. How could all the people on the street not notice a hundred cats on one building's front steps?

"Sure," Craig said, after he had looked around enough to realize he would have no immediate help in clearing the steps. "Why not?"

"Good," Mouth said. "Now, would you please apologize for striking my friend with the rock and we can have this unsightly mess settled."

"And just why should I do that?"

Craig was getting mad. Who ever heard of apologizing to a cat? This guy was totally crazy.

"Because you had no reason to strike my friend. She had done nothing to you."

"It was just a damned stray cat," Craig said. "Why are you picking on me? And besides, I can throw a rock at it if I damn well please. If I were you, I'd have these steps clear by the time I get back."

Craig spun and headed off down the street, not looking back. He'd read the paper first after all. The scratch really wasn't that bad.

All the way to the library he had the feeling he was being watched. Along the way there were a lot of cats. Many more than he had ever noticed before. But not one got close enough for him to try hitting with a rock.

Two dozen cats guarded the library steps. As Craig approached, more jumped up from the bushes.

A young couple came out of the front doors and started down the steps, seeming not to notice the unusual number of animals. The cats moved out of the couple's way and then, like water filling in behind a boat, returned to their places.

Craig stopped twenty feet in front of the steps as more and more cats joined the mass of colored fur. Then again, just as suddenly as before, the man dressed in gray appeared in place of a gray tom.

It was everything Craig could do to not run.

His stomach felt as if he'd had peppers for breakfast. He made himself take a deep breath. He could feel his heart pounding. "Just a trick. Just a trick," he repeated over and over to himself. Nothing more. Any half-baked magician could do the same stunt.

He really hadn't seen that man just grow out of that old tomcat.

"Just a trick. Just a trick."

"That was interesting," Craig finally said louder, looking up at the man in gray while trying to keep his voice as calm as he could. "How'd you do it?"

"Do what?" the man said.

"You know what I mean. How'd you just appear like that? You good at magic or something?"

The man in gray laughed a soft, slurring laugh. "You might say that."

"How'd you know where I was going? And how'd you beat me here?"

Again the man laughed. "We know all the secret ways and we always know what humans are thinking. If you had spent any time around us, you would have known that without asking."

"Sure you do," Craig said. "And I'm the Pope."

He started for the library steps. A bunch of damn cats and a crazy man weren't going to stop him.

The cats closed ranks and then, as a unit, looked up at Craig.

A wall of clear, hard ice dropped between Craig and those steps.

The coldness in the cats' eyes stopped him and then drove him staggering back, until finally, they looked away. Craig again found himself sweating in the warm summer air.

"Would you please apologize?" the man said, "So that we may all move along."

"And just what will happen if I don't?"

The man shook his head. "It would not be pleasant. Have you ever watched one of us catch a rat?"

Craig nodded. He'd watched a cat on his uncle's farm keep a field mouse running in circles for most of one afternoon.

The man in gray smiled. "Good, for it is our greatest sport. My brother, Claws That Dig, actually kept a rat trapped, but alive, for two full days before the rat died of heart failure. My brother is much honored."

"You're crazy," Craig said and spun away before any of the cats could look up at him. He headed back toward his apartment at a brisk walk, restraining himself from breaking into a run.

Along the way cats paced ahead and behind him, just out of his throwing range.

Cats covered Craig's apartment building's steps as he got in sight.

A large gray tom sat in the middle of them, calmly gazing up the street away from Craig, as if all the sights in the world were in that direction.

Craig had decided he was just going to plow right into the middle of them without stopping. He might get a cut or two, but he would show them who was the strongest. They would just scatter and run and he'd be done with them.

By the time he was twenty steps away, a hundred cats had joined ranks against him.

At five steps away, they all looked up at him.

This time the ice wall of their eyes smashed into Craig like a steel door slammed in his face.

The next thing he knew he was sitting dazed on the sidewalk looking up at the cats and the man dressed in gray.

"It would take a simple apology," the man said. "Nothing more. This is your last chance."

Craig stumbled to his feet and brushed off the seat of his pants. He was getting damn mad. All he wanted to do was go into his apartment and put some disinfectant on a cut. Now some crazy man and a bunch of trained cats were playing games with him. No one did that to Craig Lieberman and got away with it.

If this guy wanted to play, Craig would play. Only Craig had the law on his side and it was about time he had this Mouth guy arrested. Then Craig would see just who would apologize.

Without a word, Craig turned and headed up the street toward the Thirty-first Precinct.

And again, the cats paced him on all sides.

Craig could feel his stomach tightening as he kept telling himself he was just being foolish. A bunch of cats couldn't hurt him. They certainly couldn't act together.

It was just a trick.

Nothing more.

Fifty to sixty of the cats beat him to the police station.

They sat on the front steps of the busy station, moving only to watch something unseen in the distance or get out of the way of the people going in and out. None of the police seemed to notice anything odd, and a few people stopped to pet the large gray tom who sat up on the stone balustrade to the right of the door.

Craig strode toward the steps. There was no way they could stop him now. They wouldn't dare with all these people around. Just let one of them stray within kicking distance of his foot and they'd see just who should apologize.

Damn stupid animals.

Three paces short of the bottom step, Craig again slammed into the ice wall of their combined stare as in unison they turned to look at him.

Two

"YOU ALL RIGHT, mister?" The cop asked as he held Craig's arm and helped him sit up.

"I think so," Craig said and nodded, then quickly reached for the bump on the back of his head as sharp stabbing pains shot through his skull.

"Banged your head on the concrete pretty damn hard," the cop said, keeping his grip tight on Craig's left arm. "You sure you're all right?"

Craig let the cop help him back to his feet and hold on to him as Craig dusted off his pants.

"I'm fine," Craig said. "But don't you think you should do something about getting rid of all those cats?" Craig pointed at the steps.

The cop looked up at where Craig indicated. "You mean that old gray fellow? Hell, why would we want to do that?"

Even through the pain from the back of his head, Craig understood that he had to be careful. Real careful, or seeing all these cats was going to get him thrown into the nut house. Then he'd really hear the cats laughing.

"It must be the whack on the head," Craig said, holding the lump on his head. "But I'm seeing about fifty cats there on the precinct steps. How many are you seeing?"

The cop laughed, but still didn't let go of Craig's arm. "Only one, mister. You better get to a Doc and get yourself checked out. You went straight over backwards. Damn lucky you didn't kill yourself. You want me to get you a ride down to the emergency room?"

Craig nodded, then winced at the pain the movement caused. "Sure. I could use a lift." That would at least get him away from the cats and give him time to think. How could cats be invisible? It wasn't possible. Maybe he was sicker than he thought he was. Maybe he should have the doctor give him a good checkup. Never hurt to be careful.

"This way," the cop said and pointed at a patrol car sitting in front of the station. Two dozen cats blocked the passenger side of the car and others were moving slowly in that direction. They weren't going to let him in the car. And right now his head hurt too much to fight it.

"On second thought, I think I'll just walk home. I live close by. Thanks." Craig pulled away from the policeman and started back up the street.

This time even more cats paced along on all sides of him. Four different

times Craig tried ducking suddenly into restaurants or shops, but cats filled the doors as if they knew what he was planning. Maybe they did know what he was thinking.

That just didn't seem possible.

He tried hailing a cab, but cats moved between him and the curb and he didn't dare go near the street.

A hundred cats covered the steps of his apartment building. He tried standing back and throwing rocks into the middle of the mass of fur, but after the first rock, which fell short, every time he'd raise his hand to throw, a cat jumped out of nowhere and clawed painfully at the back of his leg.

Finally, after both his pant legs were torn and one ankle was bleeding, he gave up, crossed the street, and sat on the bus stop bench facing his apartment.

He watched as his neighbors moved up and down through the cats without seeming to notice them. Why were the cats doing this to him? He'd only thrown a little rock. A cat had scratched him first. Why didn't they just leave him alone? Or find someone else?

During the next hour he made a dozen more attempts at getting inside buildings, restaurants, or cabs. All were blocked.

Craig even tried telling a cop, but like the first, the policeman just laughed.

Finally, Craig decided the quickest way out was to apologize. He'd get even later, but right now all he wanted to do was go inside. He was getting hungry.

As he slowly approached the steps, the man appeared in place of the gray tom.

Craig fought down the urge to run. "I'm ready to apologize now," he said, keeping his gaze turned away from the gray man.

"It's much too late for that," the man said. "You were given your chance. Three of them to be exact."

"Wait just a minute," Craig said and took a step forward. "I didn't do anything that bad to you or your friends. I'm sorry I threw that rock, so let's just forget it? All right?"

"I'm afraid not," the man said. "We are hunters. We do not make it a practice to let prey go just because they whimper."

"Whimper!" Craig took another step closer. "Come down here and I'll show you whimper."

"We shall see," the man in gray said, and then smiled, "just who will show who."

Craig looked quickly around. There must be a good two hundred cats sitting on the steps and along both sides of the street. He wouldn't stand a chance if he pushed it now.

He turned back to the man dressed in gray, took a deep breath, and tried to calm down. "Answer me one question. Why me? Why pick on me and let all of these other people alone?"

"Because you let us catch you," the man said. "We gave you every chance to get away. As with any prey, only the stupid or the slow get caught. I think in human terms it is called survival of the fittest."

"I'm as fit as anyone," Craig yelled at the man in gray, then whirled around and headed back across the street to the bench to plan his next move.

On the top step of the apartment building, the gray tom dozed in the warm afternoon sun.

Three

CRAIG SPENT THE night on the bench across the street from his apartment. Hunger cut ribbons from the insides of his stomach and he felt dizzy most of the morning.

The mass of cats never left the apartment steps or the surrounding doorways.

At seven a.m. he tried to sneak around to the back door of the building, but dozens of cats blocked the alley.

By two in the afternoon, he had again tried getting into nearby buildings, restaurants, and a dozen passing cabs.

Three times he had ended up on the sidewalk with another bump on the back of his head and a headache that made him cry.

Each time, the passersby just walked around him as if he wasn't there. No one stopped to help him, or even give him a second glance.

Not even the cops spoke to him any more.

Somehow, the cats had made him invisible.

He tried walking at his apartment steps with his eyes closed, thinking that if he couldn't see the cats, they wouldn't be able to drop their wall in front of him.

It didn't work.

Their ice wall felt as solid as a brick building. He didn't know how long he was out cold after that attempt.

By six p.m., the hunger was more than he could stand.

He went back across the street to try pleading with the man in gray.

The man wouldn't appear.

The old gray tom just lay on the top step and stared off down the street as if it couldn't even hear Craig yelling.

That night, Craig again slept on the bench across the street from his apartment.

Four

HUNGER, THIRST, AND HEAT pounded at Craig like hammers against a block of ice.

Parts of his sanity shattered and melted with every passing hour.

At ten in the morning, he tried to throw himself into the middle of the street in front of a passing wave of traffic.

Two dozen cats stopped him at the curb.

At noon, he tried to pick up a garbage can and hit a policewoman with it. He was unconscious for over two hours.

At seven, in front of his own apartment building, he got down on his knees on the hot pavement and begged the assembled masses of cats to give him something to drink.

Not one cat even so much as looked at him.

He spent that night stretched out against the curb in front of his apartment steps.

Five

THREE DOZEN CATS slowly herded Craig Leiberman into a dead-end alley two blocks from his apartment building. It took them most of the day, as they continually had to wait for Craig to regain consciousness.

The back doors of the kitchens of three restaurants fed out onto the alley, filling the dark space between the buildings with a thick smorgasbord of smells.

Craig sat against a brick wall and drank in the odors as ten cats guarded each door.

Craig twice attempted to get at the garbage from the three restaurants. While a dozen cats stood guard, a yellow tabby and a white and gray female cat sat on top of the dumpster and clawed at Craig's hands every time he reached forward.

After the second attempt, his hands were bleeding so much, he sucked at his own blood to get moisture for his cracked mouth and lips.

Six

ON THE SIXTH day, except for one attempt to crawl down the alley, Craig Lieberman lay unconscious in the dirt of the alley.

Six cats took turns guarding him.

On the morning of the seventh day, a gray tom cat walked slowly, lazily up the alley to the body of Craig Lieberman and sniffed at his torn shirt sleeve.

Then, without hesitation, the cat raised its paw and sharply hit the man on the cheek, leaving four evenly spaced claw marks.

The man didn't move.

The old cat studied the man for a moment, then turned and strolled back up the empty alley.

Three blocks away, a construction worker named Burt Hopkins went to pet a large yellow cat that had strayed onto their work sight. The cat scratched the worker's hand and then quickly dodged Burt's kick.

And the sport began again.

~

DEAN WESLEY SMITH

USA TODAY BESTSELLING AUTHOR

LIFE
of a
DREAM

**A SCIENCE FICTION NOVEL
OF LIFE, OF LOVE,
AND HOLDING ON TO BOTH**

USA Today *bestselling writer, Dean Wesley Smith, finally gives popular Captain Brian Saber his first full-length novel.*

Brian Saber and Dot Leeds constantly must leave their nursing home rooms and fly across known space to save the Earth and the Earth Protection League. They love the job, the love feeling needed.

But in the end, will being needed be enough?

A novel of hope and a future.

LIFE OF A DREAM
An Earth Protection League Novel

For Kris
Who is putting up with me getting older between every mission.

Author's Note

Early parts of this novel are new and altered variations of four short stories. I liked how Brian and Dot's stories evolved in the stories, so I decided to include the stories in altered form instead of telling it again. The four stories are: "The Gift of a Dream," "Hand and Space," "A Time to Dream," and "We Dream of a Moon."

The First Mission

One

December 24th, 2018
Actual Earth Time
Location: Chicago

DOROTHY "DOT" LEEDS pulled herself slowly up to a sitting position, using the metal railing on her nursing home bed. The railing was cold in her hand and the room felt like it had a chill to it. She rubbed her old legs through her thin cotton nightgown, slowly, as if doing so would bring back some of the long, lost feeling to them. She had been dreaming again. Dreaming of dancing, as she and her husband used to do every Saturday night.

Like him, and most of the use of her legs, those days were long gone.

Yet every night, without fail, she dreamed of dancing. Usually the dream was of a small dance floor just big enough to swirl around. Often she was with her dead husband, Dave. Sometimes she was with a handsome man she couldn't exactly see clearly.

She could never really see the dancehall or who was watching around the edges. It was a dream and those people didn't matter.

Moving, dancing was all that was important. She loved the feeling of almost flying around the floor, the strong grip of her partner helping her float like a bird on a soft wind.

In this reality, at her advanced age, she was far from a bird in any form.

Around her, the Shady Valley Nursing Home was quiet.

The Christmas festive decorations filled the hall outside her open door, and later today she knew there'd be ham for Christmas Eve dinner. She had enjoyed that ham dinner for years now and actually looked forward to it, since the ham was always moist and soft and allowed her old teeth to chew it easily.

Then there would be turkey tomorrow for Christmas dinner. Sometimes they overcooked the turkey and it was tough, other times it had been moist and the dressing wonderful. The same two meals every Christmas for years now, since she had moved in here and her only son had moved from Chicago to the west coast and no longer took her out for Christmas

or Christmas Eve dinners. Now he could only afford an occasional holiday call and a once-a-year summer visit.

She knew he felt bad about missing holidays, but her time was almost gone and he had a family to spend the holidays with and enjoy. He did what he could for her, she understood that. She didn't blame him at all and even had encouraged him to stay with his family at Christmas and let her enjoy her friends here.

She took a deep breath and kept rubbing her legs, slowly, trying to get any kind of feeling into them.

She could hear the faint ticking of Brian Saber's old wall clock across the hall, but nothing more.

It was now Christmas Eve day, very early in the morning actually, and for some reason, Christmas Eve always seemed to be quieter than any time of the year. Not even the snowstorm outside rattled the windows. The wind off Lake Michigan must have shifted as the weatherman on television earlier had predicted it would. It was amazing what people could do these days with science stuff.

She glanced at the blue numbers of her alarm clock. Two minutes after four in the morning.

"Oh, great, just great," she said softly to herself. It would be at least another hour before the night nurse stopped in to check on her. She was going to need to use the bathroom before then. That's what she got for having that second cup of tea. Now she was paying for it.

"Go slow," she whispered, talking to herself.

She rolled over and eased down the bar on the side of her bed, then levered herself slowly to the edge, and made sure her wheelchair was in position and the brake locked. Last thing she would need on Christmas Eve was that thing rolling away from her and her falling and breaking an old brittle bone.

Using the muscles in her stomach to control her legs, as she had taught herself to do twenty-five years ago after the car accident, she rolled on her side and moved her mostly dead legs off the edge of the bed. Then with a twist she had done hundreds of times, she half-dropped, half-lowered herself into her wheelchair.

She could still stand, still move her legs enough to shuffle, still walk in a very slow fashion with support and she did that as often as she could, but that took real focus and she felt better not trying to make it most places without sitting in the wheelchair.

Especially if she was alone like this.

The feeling of making it safely into the chair made her smile.

She often had the nurse or orderly help her out of bed just for safety, but still having the freedom to do it on her own was the most important thing she held onto.

At eighty-four years of age, freedom was everything. There sure wasn't much else.

She wheeled her chair around and headed for the bathroom.

She was halfway there when a cold draft whipped her nightgown around her legs, as if someone close by had opened a door.

Her sliding door led out to the front garden of the nursing home. It was closed and the drapes hung down limp. Her room's big metal door into the hallway was braced open as it always was at night.

She could see slightly in the faint light from the nurse's station and her nightlight in her bathroom. Nothing was out of place.

She must have imagined that or a ghost had drifted past her. So many people had died in this nursing home over the years, it wouldn't have surprised her if it was haunted.

She was about to continue on toward the restroom when she glanced out and across the hall.

There she saw a young man, shadowed and wearing some sort of dark uniform, pick eighty-five-year-old Brian Saber out of his bed and head for his room's sliding glass door. That door led outside into the cold winter night and the center courtyard of the nursing home.

There was nothing out there.

No one even went out there until the spring and summer and early fall.

At first she was stunned at what she saw.

"Get help, you idiot," she muttered. She was about to shout for the nurse when she heard Brian's distinctive laugh.

Whatever was happening, Brian was a part of it. He didn't seem to be minding at all.

Maybe it was some sort of Christmas gift from someone.

Maybe Brian's son was giving him a treat of some kind.

She knew he had one son, but they hadn't talked about him much at all, other than Brian was proud of him.

After a moment, the man carrying Brian had again opened the sliding door to Brian's room and the two of them had disappeared silently outside, leaving only a short draft of cold air behind as the door slid silently closed.

What in the world was Brian up to?

She talked with him a lot during lunches and dinners.

In fact, she considered him her best friend in the place, and if they had been younger by a few decades, she was sure they would have been having a fling, since Brian's wife had died about the same time as her husband.

Yet Brian had never mentioned doing anything like this. He seemed so down-to-earth, solid. Something crazy didn't make sense for him in her mind.

She waited, almost holding her breath in the silence of the nursing home night, then eased out into the hallway.

To her right was the bright-lit nurse's station, decorated in red ribbons and white bows. She could see the night-nurse's head sticking just above the top of the low counter. She was obviously bent over some paperwork and paying no attention at all.

Taking a deep breath, Dot silently wheeled her chair quickly the rest of the way across the hall and into Brian's room.

His bed was slept in, the blankets and sheet pushed back, his wheelchair beside his nightstand, his old wall clock ticked the seconds away.

But there was no sign of Brian.

She sat for a moment, listening to the wall clock count down the remaining time in her life.

This was so strange.

She moved to the sliding glass door that opened from his room out into a central courtyard. She pulled the curtain aside, not knowing what to expect.

There was nothing out there.

A cold Chicago night. She could almost feel the cold radiating through the glass to her thin skin. She shivered and moved closer to see where Brian had gone.

In the snow, she could see a man's tracks coming from the center of the courtyard to Brian's door, another set going back. But she couldn't see where they had gone.

Maybe through another door on the other side of the courtyard, but she had no idea why they would do that.

She had no idea why Brian would do any of this.

She eased her chair away from the window and moved it so she was sitting in the dark corner of the room.

She had a sneaking hunch Brian would be back very shortly. And she didn't plan on leaving until then, no matter how badly she needed to go to the bathroom.

Two

December 24th, 1958
Equivalent Earth Time
Location: Deep Space

CAPTAIN BRIAN SABER of the *Earth Protection League* slapped the two hot Proton Stunners into their holsters on his hips, ran a hand through his thick head of wavy brown hair, and smiled at the six dead bodies of Bocturian scum.

"I don't think you'll be sabotaging any more slow-speed Earth supply ships."

They didn't answer, for obvious reasons.

They were dead.

He felt proud, staring at the oil-smelling bodies, their tentacles twitching in the air, their six eyes staring in their death stare. They looked like a bad cross between an octopus and a pile of dog crap.

Around him the control room of their ship stank of a combination of fish and intense lilac perfume. Brothel jokes were common anytime anyone from the *Earth Protection League* had to board a Bocturian ship.

He knew for a fact that it was going to take some time before the smell got out of his leather pants, silk shirt, leather vest, and high boots. He hoped it washed out before his next mission, otherwise his crew was never going to let him forget it.

One of the pirates seemed to move and he shot it again just for good measure.

"Captain?" Carl Turner, his third in command asked over the communications link. "Are you wrapped up there?"

"Bows are tied and presents under the tree," he said, kicking each pile of pirate scum to make sure it wasn't alive. "How about the rest of the Bocturian ships?"

In this mission there had been ten *Earth Protection League* ships fighting a small fleet of Bocturian pirates. The pirates hadn't stood a chance.

"Cleaned up," Turner said.

Saber felt a slight tinge of regret. The mission was almost over. "Prepare to pick me up," he ordered. "I'm going to need a good bath before we head back to Earth."

"I copy that," Turner said. "I can smell you from here."

"Next time you do the boarding," Saber said, laughing.

Damn it felt good to be alive and needed to defend Earth.

"Uh, Captain," Turner said, "we took a slight hit to the forward section of the ship."

"Anyone hurt?"

The twisting in Saber's gut told him the answer to his question. On this mission there had been only ten of them on the ship instead of the normal thirty-eight to forty-two crew. Sometimes the ship held up to fifty crew members, but they had needed only the gunners and support crew this time, since the mission had been easy and designed to be quick.

But Saber knew that two of that small crew had been in the forward section.

"Ben and Sarah," Turner said, his voice soft and low. "Ben will survive. Sarah was killed."

"Damn, damn, damn," Saber said.

He hadn't known Sarah that well, but she had a great smile and an infectious laugh. She had barely topped five feet tall, but seemed really tough. They had been on six missions together, with her working weapons for him on two of the last three. He didn't even know what part of Earth she was from, or how old she was back there. But if she did have some family, they weren't going to have a happy Christmas Eve.

"Inform command and medical," Saber said.

"Copy that," Turner said.

With one more kick at the closest of the dead pirates, Saber turned and headed for the airlock.

Twenty minutes later, after a quick shower, he was standing over the coffin-like bed of his sleep chamber.

He had already tossed his uniform into the cleaning bins to be laundered when they returned to Earth, and had pulled his nursing home nightshirt over his young body. It always felt weird doing that, yet he knew that on the other end of the flight having the nightshirt on was better than having one of the young soldiers dress him.

He sighed and stared at the sleep chamber. The problems with Trans-Galactic flight were the reasons he was here.

At top speeds, Trans-Galactic flight regressed a human body, so for T-G jumps to the outer limits of the *Earth Protection League* borders, they had to use old people to start.

He was just about as old as they came.

No one really understood exactly why T-G flight worked that way.

Or why on the return flight, they returned to their original age.

Or at least no one had been able to explain it to him in a way he understood. He knew it had something to do with relativity, the curved nature of space above the speed of light, all combined with the fixed nature of matter.

None of it made any sense to him.

All he knew was that on Earth he was an eighty-five-year-old cripple in a nursing home, trying to fight off more strokes. Out here on the borders of the *Earth Protection League* space, he was a young and healthy man again. All thanks to the nature of Trans-Galactic flight.

He climbed into the coffin-shaped sleep chamber and smoothed down his old nightshirt. Then with a sigh of resignation, he quickly pulled the lid down, triggering the departure and his quick nap.

Fighting the alien pirates had taken him three days out here. He'd be back in his room early Christmas Eve morning, less than twenty minutes after he had left.

But he'd still have the three days of fresh memories.

That was one of the good things about the relative nature of time and space and matter.

With luck, there'd be another mission this week.

And then he would have another chance to be young again, fight the good fight as a hero of the *Earth Protection League* on the very edges of civilized space.

Three

December 24th, 2018
Actual Earth Time
Location: Chicago

THE YOUNG SOLDIER picked him out of the sleep chamber as if he weighed nothing. Actually, he didn't weigh much more than a hundred pounds these days. And he ate as much as he could, but couldn't seem to put any weight on his old body.

"How'd the mission go, Captain?" the soldier asked as the tractor beam released them in the center court of the nursing home and the soldier moved with sure steps through the soft snow.

"Just about as good as could be hoped," Saber said, his breath frosting up in the cold night air. He used to love the cold, crisp Chicago nights. Now they just chilled him to his old bones, even only being out in it for fifteen seconds or so.

"Good to hear," the young man carrying him said.

Both Saber and the young soldier knew that was all Saber could tell him about the mission. Almost no one on Earth even knew about the *Earth Protection League*.

It was just safer that way.

The young soldier was a member of the *League,* of course, but unless he decided to spend twenty years on a slow shuttle that stayed under light speed, he'd never see anything beyond the moon until he got a lot older. So there was just no reason to tell him about the missions. The kid couldn't go out there. He was just too young to survive the age and time regression of the T-G flight.

The soldier carried Saber through the sliding door into his room and laid him gently in the bed.

Then the kid stepped back and saluted. "Great job, Captain. I'll see you again soon. Have a Merry Christmas."

"Thank you. You too."

The kid turned and then stopped, as if seeing a ghost.

It took Saber a moment to understand what the problem was. Then he saw Dot, the woman who lived across the hall, as she wheeled her chair out of the shadows of the corner.

Oh, no.

Saber didn't know what to think or even do. This was something he had never imagined happening.

Dot was his best friend here in the nursing home. He'd often wished he could tell her about his missions. But he was restricted from doing so by regulations.

The *EPL* had a lot of very firm regulations. Considering the nature of the job and who was doing the fighting, it had to be strict and clear.

The young soldier glanced back at him, a look of fear on his face, his hand on his gun on his hip.

Saber understood the reason for the kid's fear. If the case warranted, the young soldier was ordered to kill anyone who happened to get in the way of a mission.

Saber looked at his friend sitting there in her wheelchair clearly looking confused.

Dot wasn't in the way.

Tonight's mission was over.

"It's all right, soldier." Saber looked the young kid directly in the eyes and smiled. "She's a friend."

The young man stood for a moment, then nodded. "Understood, Captain. Command will be expecting a report on this."

"They will have it in the morning."

The young soldier nodded to Dot. "Goodnight, ma'am." He then vanished through the door, closing it behind him.

Saber lay on his back in his bed, his head turned, staring at Dot. He couldn't really see the expression on her face, and she said nothing.

He could feel his heart beating in his chest, and he hoped he still didn't smell like those aliens he had killed.

For the next few moments the silence in the room sounded like a roaring engine about to overwhelm them both, the ticking of his wall clock like the timer of a bomb.

Then finally Dot rolled a little closer to his bed and said, "Have I got you in some sort of trouble?"

Saber remembered the pitched fight he'd just had with six alien pirates, the success they had had again in defending the *Earth Protection League* and its space.

And the death of Sarah.

That was trouble.

Not this.

He laughed.

But he realized he was back in his old body and the laugh turned into a hacking, coughing, old man's laugh that lasted for a good thirty ticks of his clock before he finally stopped.

"You want to know where I was?" he asked.

She nodded.

He motioned her closer to his bed.

"You won't believe me, but I would love to tell you."

"You never know what I might believe," she said.

He laughed softly this time, avoiding the hacking cough.

"It's going to feel good to finally be able to tell you about my missions."

She nodded.

He couldn't believe it. After all the years of going out and coming back, of defending Earth against all odds, and all alien scum, he *finally* got to tell someone.

And for the next hour it felt wonderful.

Almost as good as killing those alien pirates.

Almost.

Four

December 24th, 2018
Actual Earth Time
Location: Chicago

DOT WAS MORE stunned than anything else.

Brian's wild story of being a Captain in the *Earth Protection League*, of fighting alien pirates in deep space as a young man, was outrageous to say the least.

He told her about how he had had to board a pirate ship, fight all six of them, and how bad they smelled. The details of the story were very clear, right down to how he kicked one of the dead bodies before he left the pirate ship.

She couldn't believe any of it, yet she had seen him be carried in and out of the room by a man who had called him Captain. And who wore a gun and was upset that she was there.

More than likely it was all just some wild fantasy Brian had paid a kid to help him carry out as a Christmas present to himself. After all, he'd only been gone from the room for twenty minutes, not three days like he had claimed.

Yet a part of her had wanted to believe his wild dream.

Especially the part about growing young again, because of how time and space and matter worked.

His explanation of that had almost been funny enough to laugh at. Yet when he had tried to explain it to her, she hadn't laughed. Just listened, hoping to not break the fantasy world he lived in.

She liked him enough to do that for him.

Especially on Christmas Eve.

It wasn't until the end of his wild story, after telling her about the loss of his crewmate, Sarah, that he asked her something that bothered her on a deep level. He asked if she was interested in joining up, being a soldier in the *Earth Protection League*, of being young again to help Earth fight whatever threatened its space borders.

The question bothered her a great deal, but instead of saying so, she laughed and said, "Who wouldn't like to be young again?"

"Great," he said. "I can't promise anything, but it never hurts to ask the brass in charge of it all."

At that moment, Joyce, the night nurse tonight, poked her head in and smiled at them. She asked if Brian needed anything, then winked at Dot and left.

Dot laughed and suddenly realized she hadn't yet made it to the bathroom.

"I'll see you at breakfast," she told Brian, heading for the door as fast as she could move her chair.

"Can't say anything about this to anyone," Brian said behind her.

Again she laughed as she went into the hall.

"Who would believe me?"

She didn't believe it.

Not one word of it.

But she wanted to.

Five

December 24th, 2018
Actual Earth Time
Location: Chicago

AT BREAKFAST ON Christmas Eve day, Brian was all smiles, his wheel-

chair pulled up to a table in the corner of the festively decorated lunchroom. No one else was sitting at the table.

Green and red garland hung from just about everything that wasn't needed, and the room smelled of a combination of Christmas wreathes and pancakes. Actually a pretty good smell as far as Dot was concerned.

Beyond the window, the Chicago weather had turned cold and clear, the sun almost too bright off the white ground. All the snow was going to freeze solid by the time the day was done and it got dark. It was lucky she wasn't going anywhere for Christmas tomorrow. The roads would be awful.

After all the years of living in this area, she knew that without a doubt. But she had no reason left in her life at this point to even step outside.

She had forced herself to do a little walking this morning, even though she was tired from being up so late and talking with Brian last night, so she moved along behind her wheelchair, slowing pushing it around the other tables so she could join him.

"Good morning," she said, sitting with her back to the window so she wouldn't be blinded from the bright sunlight. "Going to get cold tonight out there."

He glanced at the window behind her, then back at her, his smile growing even bigger. "I hadn't honestly noticed. But might be a problem for my son getting here later on."

She knew Brian had a son in the area, but hadn't met him in all the years they had known each other. Maybe today she would get a chance.

Brian waited for the orderly to give her some orange juice, ask if she would like her normal eggs and pancakes, and leave.

Then he leaned over slightly and whispered, "There's a mission tonight and League Command said that if I was willing to train you on the ship's proton weapons, you could join up. You would take Sarah's place. You'd be a private, but there's room for advancement."

"You're kidding, right?" Dot asked, staring at him.

He had shaved this morning, but his skin was still rough with light stubble, and there was a twinkle in his eye that she'd never seen before. "Not in the slightest," he said.

Then his expression got very serious and a coldness came into his eyes.

That made her sit back, surprised.

"But it's dangerous." His voice was a low whisper. "I won't kid you on that. You die out there and they bring your body back here and you're found dead in your sleep in the morning. The time travel part of things just doesn't revive anyone."

She hadn't been so confused in years. She took her red cloth napkin with some Christmas scene on it and unfolded it and put it on her lap to give her a moment to think.

Brian was seriously asking her to join in his delusions.

And he was telling her it was dangerous.

What were he and that friend that had carried him out going to do? Would Brian kill her if she went with them in the middle of the night?

Brian reached across and touched her hand.

She could feel the roughness of his hand against her brittle skin. It was the first time a man, other than an aide, had touched her in any way since her husband had died all those years ago.

"You said you wanted to be young again," he said, staring into her eyes with those intense brown eyes of his.

"I do," she said, moving her hand away.

"But you don't trust me, do you?" Brian said, smiling. The boyish twinkle was back in his eyes.

"Would you?" she asked. "You have to admit, your story is pretty wild stuff."

"I didn't believe it either, my first night," he said, laughing and clearly remembering something since he seemed to be looking off into the distance. After a moment he went on. "To be honest with you, even after going on more than a hundred missions, I still don't believe it."

"So I should just *trust you*?" she asked.

"How old are you, Dot?" he asked in return.

"Eighty-four," she said, squaring her shoulders. No man had asked her that question in years. She wasn't sure she liked telling a man her age. She was still very old-fashioned that way.

"I'm eighty-five," he said. "And this old body is getting worse by the day it seems. What I do for the *League* is a dream come true. At our age, what else do we have to live for but dreams?"

At that moment, for some crazy reason, she decided he was right. Maybe it was because it was Christmas Eve and there was a faint Christmas song playing in the background and the sun was shining and she would have no family visiting today.

"To be honest with you, even after going on more than a hundred missions, I still don't believe it."

Or just maybe she really didn't have anything to lose.

Either way she'd play along with him and his wild fantasy, maybe even let herself believe that she might be young again for a short time.

Every night she dreamed of dancing anyway. Why not join Brian in his dreams for a night?

"I'll go," she said, smiling at him.

The light in his eyes was like a child seeing the presents under a Christmas tree. She knew she had made the right decision.

With that the orderly brought their breakfast and they talked about family and Christmas memories.

And at lunch they sat together and did the same, sharing the past with each other. Dot learned more about Brian that day than she had in years. It seemed that because she was willing to go with him, he felt more open with her.

And she felt more open with him for some reason.

She really had made the right decision, she knew that.

She went to bed at her normal time of eight and managed to doze, but awoke at midnight, worried that she had made a really stupid decision.

She could hear Brian's clock ticking and not much else. The worry about what was going to happen kept her awake far too long and she kept waking up at any sound.

At one point she almost wheeled across the hall and told Brian to forget about her going along, but before she could get up enough energy to do that, she had just gone back to sleep, deciding she would deal with it in the morning.

It was three in the morning, Christmas morning, when the young woman dressed in black came across the hall from Brian's room.

Dot heard her coming because Brian had laughed.

Dot was suddenly scared out of her wits.

But the fact that there was a young woman also involved calmed her a little. It wasn't just Brian and some friend of his.

"My name is Lieutenant Sherri," the woman said, stopping beside her bed and smiling. "Brian says you're thinking of joining the League, Mrs. Leeds. I sure envy you."

Those words rocked Dot completely out of her fear, which drained away like someone had pulled a plug in a sink.

She looked up into the young dark eyes and the smiling face of Lieutenant Sherri over her bed. "Envy me? Why?"

"Because you get to go out there, into space, to defend Earth. It will be years before I can go, even on a short-run mission."

Dot only nodded.

She had no idea what the young woman had said or meant. And she still didn't believe she was going into space, but at this point she really didn't know what to believe was going to happen. But at least the fear was gone.

"Are you ready?" the young woman asked as she moved in beside Dot's bed and lowered the railing.

"Why not?" Dot said. "After all, it's Christmas morning."

The woman picked her up as easily as the orderly, stepped to the door and glanced down the hall to make sure the nurse wasn't watching. Then quickly, she carried Dot across the hall and into Brian's room.

Brian was already gone and the young woman carrying her didn't hesitate. She went right through Brian's open sliding glass door and out into the cold night air, her feet crunching on the frozen snow, her arms holding Dot gently, but firmly.

"Aren't I going to be missed?" Dot asked as the night air bit at her, sharp, pin-like. Not in a million years had she expected to go out into this cold night air.

"You'll be back in twenty minutes," the young woman said. "Everything is taken care of on this end."

"We won't be outside that long, will we?" Dot asked, starting to shiver. The older she had gotten, the more sensitive she had become to the cold. This was like a knife cutting at her skin.

"Only a moment," Lieutenant Sherri said.

The rest went like a blur for Dot.

One moment they were in the cold, then she and the woman carrying her were floating up through the air into something big above her in the night sky. That was a nightmare and Dot wanted to close her eyes, but didn't.

The minute they lifted off the ground, she started to really believe Brian's story.

And suddenly she was scared again.

The young Lieutenant Sherri walked her quickly down a hallway that looked like it could be a hallway on a cruise liner. Then she carried Dot into a single room.

The coffin-like sleep chamber in the small room was exactly like Brian had described.

Lieutenant Sherri laid her in the deep chamber, on the soft padding, and then pointed to a closet. "Your uniform is in there, made to fit you exactly. When you wake up, just shove the lid open and get dressed."

"How will I get out of this?" Dot asked, indicating the sleep chamber. She knew without a doubt she was too weak to push herself over the edge of something this deep.

The young lieutenant just laughed softly and then said with a smile, "Just trust me, you won't have any trouble."

With that the lieutenant closed the lid.

Before Dot could even think another thought or begin to panic, she was asleep.

Six

December 25th, 1956
Equivalent Earth Time
Location: Deep Space

DOT DIDN'T DREAM, or at least she didn't remember dreaming.

She awoke without opening her eyes.

She was almost afraid to.

She could feel the softness of the padding under her, so she knew she wasn't in her own bed in the nursing home.

She could remember clearly the frightening moments of floating through the air above the Shady Valley Nursing Home and seeing the Chicago skyline out over the cold, clear winter's night.

Slowly, she opened her eyes to see the top of the lid of the sleep chamber. There was a faint light coming from around the edge and the top seemed much farther away than it actually was, more likely to keep down claustrophobia.

She raised a hand and pushed the lid open, then stared at the skin on her bare arm.

Young skin.

Perfect skin, not the blemished, dried skin of an eighty-four year old woman.

Was that even possible?

Then she moved her leg.

It was as if her heart stopped at that moment.

Her breath caught and she wasn't sure if she was going to burst into tears.

Not since the accident that had killed her husband and crippled her had she been able to move her legs without a lot of work after waking up.

Yet now she could.

Both of them.

Easily.

She sat up and watched her legs move under her old nightgown.

Not possible, but she needed to really test this.

Quickly, not allowing herself to think about it, she swung herself up and out of the sleep chamber, landing on the floor, *on her feet*, as if she'd done that every day for years.

Now she really did feel like crying.

For a moment she just stood there shaking.

Brian had been telling the truth.

Or this really was the most vivid dream she had ever had.

She touched her own soft skin on her arms. It didn't feel like she was dreaming.

She glanced around.

She was alone in what looked to be a small cabin of a ship, the only furniture a bolted down chair and the coffin-like sleep chamber. This was the same room the woman had carried her into.

Dot quickly pulled off her nightgown and studied herself in a full-length mirror that was bolted to the back of the closet door.

It was her young body, all right. From her eighty-four year old mind, it looked perfect, even though she knew that in her twenties, she had thought her body far from perfect.

How little she had known then. She was one damn fine-looking broad, as they used to say.

That thought made her laugh. Her voice was higher and clearer to her ears than she remembered.

If she was going insane or this was some sort of trick, it was a great trick.

Then she opened the closet and started to get dressed.

As Lieutenant Sherri had said it would, the uniform fit perfectly.

How had anyone known her size when she was in her twenties?

The uniform consisted of undergarments that seemed very modern. White underwear and what seemed like a "sports bra" of some sort. She had never worn one, but she had heard of them. It felt far more comfortable than the old-fashioned things she wore most days.

There were brown leather pants, tall black boots, a silk blouse that fit loosely over the middle and tightly across her chest, and a leather vest with a triangle insignia on it that read *EPL*.

Earth Protection League.

So far everything Brian had told her was coming true.

How was any of this possible?

She studied herself in the mirror one more time. Never in her faintest memory did she look this good.

She turned and headed for the door, smiling, enjoying the feel of her feet solidly under her as she walked. The boots fit her feet perfectly, almost like a second skin.

It was time to see just exactly what this dream was all about before she woke up.

The door to her room slid open.

In the wide corridor on the other side two men stood, leaning against the wall. The corridor was painted a tan color with a rubber matting on the floor. Not like anything she had seen before.

One of the men was short, with light-brown hair and an infectious grin.

The other was a tall, square-shouldered, square jawed man with a handsome face and a thick head of wavy, brown hair.

They both looked to be in their early twenties and had on the same uniform as she did, only the tall, good-looking one had two weapons on his hips like an old gunslinger in the Wild West.

He pushed himself away from the wall with the ease of a man perfectly in touch with his body, then said, "Merry Christmas and welcome to my ship, *The Bad Business,* Private Dot Leeds. This is Lieutenant Carl Turner, my third in command."

Carl stuck out his hand, smiling. "Glad you decided to join us."

She nodded as she shook his hand, then glanced at the one who had introduced them.

She knew who he was, but for some reason her mind wasn't letting her admit it.

Was it really possible?

Finally, she asked, "Brian?"

He laughed, deep and rich and full of power. "Of course, but I'm afraid we have to be a little more formal on board ship. You need to call me Captain when we're on a mission like this."

She knew she was standing there, on her own two legs, her head shaking, completely stunned. More than likely her mouth was open, too.

Both men had the decency to not laugh out loud at her.

Captain Brian Saber smiled and touched her arm. His touch was almost shocking. Again, he was the only man except an orderly or nurse or doctor who had touched her in any way in decades.

"As I told you back at breakfast," Brian said, "I still think this is all a dream, too. But I'm afraid it's not."

His face got very serious and the cold, intense look she had seen in the nursing home was now in full force on this younger version. "You're going to get a quick dunk in the deep end with this mission, I'm afraid. We don't have much time."

"Why?" she managed to ask. "What do I need to do?"

"I've got to get back to the command center," Brian said. "Carl will get you checked out on the Photon Projector Beam weapons and what the enemy ships look like, and how to destroy them."

"Enemy?" she asked.

Now she was suddenly afraid again. She had never fired a weapon before and she didn't know if she could ever do it, let alone kill something.

Brian touched her shoulder in a reassuring way and it did calm her down a little.

"Good luck and I'll see you after it's all over."

With that, he turned and strode down the corridor, a man completely in charge of his world.

She watched him walk away. She had no idea that Brian had such force inside of him. At the age of eighty-five, such force was often hidden, or pounded out of a person.

She wondered how people saw her at eighty-four.

She took a deep breath, forcing herself to calm down, and turned to Carl's smiling face. "Well, show me what to do and how to do it and I'll see if I can carry my weight."

He laughed. "The Captain said you'd be a good addition to the crew. I think he just might be right."

"He did, huh?" she asked, glancing back in the direction that Captain Brian Saber had gone, as Carl led her off in the opposite direction. "Nice to know."

Then all the way down the corridor, she rejoiced in the feeling of actually walking without support again.

At one point she almost started skipping but managed to restrain herself.

Dream or no dream, simply walking again was the best Christmas present she could have ever asked for.

Seven

December 25th, 1956
Equivalent Earth Time
Location: Deep Space

THE COMMAND CENTER of *The Bad Business* was a picture of efficiency of design. Brian occupied the big center chair facing a wall of screens, controls and computer pads covering both arms of the big chair. He was the pilot and he could make his ship almost dance from that chair.

The Command Center was actually fairly small, with only four stations. Marian Knudson, a stunning redhead from Wisconsin, sat in the chair to his left, tucked up under a wide board of control panels and display screens. She did everything, often a half second of when

Brian needed it, as if she could read his mind.

In the chair to his right was Carl Turner, the best navigator in the fleet. And one of the smartest people Brian had ever met.

Brian loved this small command center more than any place he had ever been in his entire life. It was the brains and heart of a very powerful warship, sitting in the top of the head of the bird-shaped ship. He liked the electronics smell, the sounds of faint alarms as systems went through checklists, and he really loved the feel of the thick, leather chair that perfectly fit his young form.

But at this moment, all three of them were moving as fast as they could as he took his ship through and at the enemy as hard and as fast as *The Bad Business* would go.

The Astra Warsticks were long, thin things that resembled a straw with something stuck in both ends more than a spaceship. At full length, they were about the same length as his ship, and very deadly.

He dove in again at one of them, twisting to give his gunners open shots, then quickly used evasive maneuvers to avoid getting hit by the Warstick Slicing Energy Beam weapons that shot from each end of their ships like orange fluid blown out of a drinking straw.

He was trying to do everything in his power to make this a fight, but he doubted it would last long.

"Damn," Carl muttered under his breath on Saber's right as Saber barely avoided flying directly into one of the energy beams from a Warstick.

Damn was right. That had been too close. He swung the ship out wide and made a pass along the length of a turning Warstick, letting his gunners hammer at it.

Commander Marian Knudson, his second in command, sat silently on his left, her red hair pulled back off her face, her fingers dancing over the control board, making sure that he had all the information and was in contact with all the other ships at any moment, knowing where they all were.

The three of them, the only three in the control room, worked like a single person. They had done over twenty missions together and really liked each other.

But little good that was going to do them today.

Brian knew that no one at *Earth Protection League* Command thought he, or the other twenty *EPL* ships sent to this battle, would survive.

The Astra had decided to take six *League* systems. They had given Earth ten hours to turn them over, and when Earth had said no, the Astra had sent two hundred Warsticks across the border.

Saber and the other *EPL* ship's job was simply to slow the Astra down while the *League* mounted a better, and more powerful defense closer to the threatened systems.

Saber guessed the *League* figured that twenty ships full of old, nursing home residents were expendable when it came to defending Earth's space.

And Saber agreed.

He and the rest *were* expendable when it came down to fighting off the alien scum and protecting Earth and its allies.

But Brian didn't plan on getting killed or even beaten up just yet, especially by an alien that looked more like a piece of straw than an alien warrior.

But at the moment, that was exactly what was happening. From Marian's report, the *EPL* ships had managed to destroy six of the Warsticks, but had lost three of their ships in the process.

They were going to slow the Warstick fleet down, that was for sure, but they weren't going to stop it by a long ways, unless he came up with something fast.

Suddenly the voice of Dot came over the ship's communications link. "Captain?"

"Go ahead, Private," he said.

His stomach twisted and he felt sick. In the battle he had forgotten she was even on board. What a mission to be her first. And most likely her last. If they were killed, Shady Valley Nursing Home would have two deaths in one Christmas morning.

"Our weapons are doing no good against the sides of these ships," Dot said. "But I have an idea that is pretty far-fetched."

"Anything at this point," he said, moving the ship barely out of the way of two closing Warsticks trying to trap him between their open ends.

"From what the Lieutenant told me," she said, "the Warstick control room is near one end, their engine room is near the other, and weapons are fired from both ends."

"Got it right," Saber said. "What's your idea?"

"I think if you cut one of those sticks in half," she said, "you might put it out of business."

"And how would you suggest we do that?" Saber asked. Then almost before the question was out of his mouth, he knew the answer.

"Ram it," he said.

At the same moment she said, "Ram it."

"Great idea, Private," he said, suddenly feeling like they just might have a chance. A slim chance on a crazy idea, but it just might work.

He went to ship-wide com. "I want all weapons aimed forward and firing. On my mark."

The Warsticks were very thin right at the center, so the Earth ships had a

---

complete advantage in size. And the Earth ships had great forward screens since they flew so fast through space with the Trans-Galactic drive.

In fact, at full T-G drive speed, the ship could punch a hole through a small moon and come out the other side. But this close they wouldn't be able to get to full speed or full screens that only came up at higher speeds.

He swung the ship around and headed for the center of the nearest Warstick.

One problem the sticks had was turning quickly and he stayed easily ahead of the Warstick's evasive turn.

"Asteroid deflectors and shields on full!" Brian ordered.

"Already on," Carl said.

"Brace for impact!" Marian announced to the entire crew.

It was almost anticlimactic.

The ship didn't even bump. Saber had felt a worse impact running over a jackrabbit with a car back in Idaho when he was younger.

But the Warstick was cut in half. The two halves spinning away from the collision point.

A moment later, both ends of the enemy Warstick exploded in bright white flashes.

"Well, I'd say that worked," Carl said, looking over and smiling at Brian.

"I'll be a blonde," Marian said, her favorite phrase of surprise. Considering her bright red hair, that just wasn't ever possible, which is why the statement worked.

"Inform the other ships," Brian ordered. "Weapons crew, keep firing forward. Let's take out another one."

He swung the ship around and plowed through the center of another Warstick before it could even begin to turn out of his way.

The same thing happened.

They went through the alien ship as if it wasn't even there, then the separated halves of the Warstick exploded.

Maybe, just maybe, they had a chance in this fight. For the first time in a few hours, he was starting to hope he might see one more Christmas turkey dinner at the nursing home.

And with luck he would see Dot again. If they survived this, he had a surprise for her that he had been thinking about long before he invited her to join the *League.*

Two hours of hard fighting later, the Astra Warstick fleet, or what was left of it, turned and headed back for the border. There were still fifteen of the twenty Earth Protection League ships left.

They had won and won easily.

Brian reported to League Command what had happened, then sat back in his chair and took a long, deep breath. He had been sweating for hours and could desperately use a shower. He could feel himself sticking to his shirt and his chair.

But he hadn't felt this good about a mission in a long, long time.

"Nice flying, Captain," Carl said, also slouching in his chair, clearly as exhausted as Brian felt. But he had a huge smile on his tired face.

"That was almost fun," Marian said, sighing as well. "Let's not do it again for a few years, okay?"

"Agreed," Brian said, thinking about how Dot must be feeling right now. "I think this deserves a party, don't you?"

"I think the fact that we're still alive deserves something," Carl said, laughing.

"I will even drink to that," Marian said.

"Oh, God," Carl said, "a drunk redhead. That's what we need."

"Exactly what the Captain ordered," Brian said, laughing along with his two command crew.

Saber flicked the communication switch to the members of his crew. "Congratulations people, on a job well done. And special thanks to our newest crew member, Private Dot Leeds. Party in one hour, everyone. Don't be late."

Eight

December 25th, 1956
Equivalent Earth Time
Location: Deep Space

DOT SMILED AT the Captain's words and for the first time in two hours let go of the control stick for the Proton Projector Beam weapon, then sat back in her padded chair.

She couldn't remember the last time she had felt so tired and so exhilarated at the same time.

The battle had seemed to go on forever. Flashing ship after flashing ship, at times she didn't know what to fire at and

when. But she didn't think she fired at any *EPL* ships.

They were pretty amazing-looking, designed like big birds and she now knew Brian and Carl were in the command area in what looked like the top of the head.

At first she didn't think she could fire a weapon, but then she started to learn quickly when she saw the alien ships that looked like thin hourglasses. She had broken an hourglass timer once when cooking back when she was married and that's what had given her the idea to break the two ends in half.

From there the battle seemed like it had just started and then it ended.

Behind her, Private Becky Pollard came up and patted her on the back.

Becky was a stout woman with a bright smile. She had been the gunner behind Dot and to the right.

"Nice job. Much better than my first time out here."

"Thanks," Dot said, standing and stretching muscles that back in the nursing home she could barely move.

Becky was shorter than Dot's five-four, with blonde hair and freckles. During the battle she swore more than any person Dot had ever heard, using

words Dot had never dreamed a woman could use so effectively.

"I had no idea what I was doing," Dot said.

"How could you?" Becky asked, laughing with a throaty sound that seemed to be both natural and from too many cigarettes. "Remember where you were when the Captain asked you to join the crew."

"A nursing home wheelchair," Dot said, smiling and shaking her head as the memories flooding back in.

And the questions came back as well about this all being a dream. It didn't feel much like a dream anymore, that was for sure.

"Being in a nursing home sure trains you to fire a Proton Projector Beam weapon, doesn't it?" Becky said.

"I wish I had one for a few of the day nurses," Dot said.

Becky snorted and then laughed again. "Yeah, I know that feeling. Come on, I'll show you where a shower is, and you should have another fresh uniform in your room."

"Thanks," Dot said. Then, almost as if it had been a habit for the past twenty-five years, she took the first step.

And then she remembered that before this trip, she couldn't walk well and without work. And hadn't been able to for over twenty-five years.

This was a dream.

It had to be.

One hour later, freshly showered and still marveling at her ability to walk like a young person, she joined the rest of the crew in the mess area.

The place was about the twice the size of a large living room and smelled of fresh bread. It was larger by about half than the lunchroom at Shady Valley.

All the tables had been pushed against the walls leaving the smooth floor open in the middle. The crew of about forty or so milled around the outside, smiling and laughing.

She couldn't believe it. All of those young people around here were really old people back on Earth.

Drinks and food filled one table near the door, and she took a bottle of water and some fresh bread.

Becky came over and introduced her to about ten of the crew members who all seemed pleased to meet her. When they gave their names, they also gave their town. She liked that.

Finally she moved over to Captain Brian Saber who was talking with a red-head that someone said was Commander Marian Knudson, his second in command.

"Thanks for the great idea of ramming the Warsticks," he said, taking her bottle of water and handing her a drink that looked like a cross between a screwdriver and something with red juice in it. "You saved all of our lives."

She laughed. "You'd have thought of it eventually."

"Maybe, maybe not," he said. "No one in any battle with the Warsticks has ever thought of it in years. So thanks."

"You're welcome."

She knew her face was red, but she ignored the feeling and sipped at the drink, loving the sweet flavor mixed with the orange juice.

She couldn't believe she was standing, talking with Brian, on a ship that looked like a big bird, after a battle with aliens. Now she understood why she hadn't believed him when he told her about his last mission.

She didn't believe she was here, to be honest.

The Captain turned to Carl who looked like he was drinking straight scotch and said, "Fire it up."

"You got it, Captain," Carl said, smiling at her before moving away.

Carl tapped a button on a wall and music filled the room.

Christmas music, just soft enough to talk over, yet loud enough to hear clearly.

The song was an old Benny Goodman Christmas song she couldn't remember the title to, but she had loved to dance to it back when she was young. It had been an old song then, but she hadn't cared.

The Captain bowed to her slightly. "I remember in one of our lunch conversations you mentioned how much you liked to dance. And you mentioned this song. So I figured what better thing to do on Christmas than dance?"

For a moment she was sure she would wake up and lose the entire dream.

But she didn't.

She stayed right there, standing on her own two feet.

The music swirled around her, the handsome man smiled at her, the room felt perfect.

"I'd love to," she managed to say to the Captain.

She handed her drink to Marian who smiled and nodded to her.

Captain Brian Saber, the most handsome man she could ever remember seeing, took her hand and stepped to the middle of the open floor.

A moment later they were moving around the floor of the mess hall as the other crew members watched and clapped along with the music.

She was dreaming.

And it was wonderful.

And she didn't care.

All she focused on was his firm grasp, his strong muscles under his silk shirt, and his twinkling eyes and infectious smile.

She could do this all night.

Four hours later, after more dances than she could remember, she was standing beside the coffin-like sleep chamber again in the cabin they had assigned her.

She had put on the old nightgown over her young body. She knew she had to get in the chamber, but she didn't want to.

She stood there, swaying back and forth, trying to get the memory of the dancing, of just standing, clearly in her mind.

And the memory of being held by Captain Brian Saber.

She really, really needed to remember this dream.

Finally, when the warning bell rang, she had no choice.

With one last twirl on her feet, she crawled in and pulled the cover closed over her head.

The next thing she remembered, Lieutenant Sherri, dressed in black, was picking her up out of the sleep chamber and taking her down into the courtyard, floating in the cold Chicago night air.

A few minutes later, the lieutenant put her down in her wheelchair, saluted, and left.

Dot looked at her old, wrinkled hands in the dim light, then felt the deadness in her legs.

Had she been dancing on those legs?

Had it really happened?

Had she just dreamed it all?

It had been a wonderful dream. The battle had been scary, but the dancing and being young had been more than she could have ever imagined.

She needed to try to find out the answer to those questions.

She moved her chair out across the hall and through Brian's door.

He was in bed, his head turned so that he could see her as she rolled up beside him.

Even in the dim light, she could see his smile and the twinkle in his eyes.

"You've got a lot of explaining to do," she said, "before I'm really going to believe that all happened."

He laughed, managing to not cough. "I felt exactly the same way at first. And every time I end up back here in this old worthless body, I wonder if I actually did everything I remember doing."

"So it was real?" she asked, looking around the nursing home room, so far from the ship on the edge of the borders between Earth's space and other alien races. The room was in a faint light from the hall and the nightlight in the bathroom. The big wall clock ticked, filling the room with a constant reminder that time was moving forward.

This was so far from the battle with the Warsticks.

"Very real," Brian said. "And very important. We're the only ones that can go out there and defend this planet. We're the only ones old enough to withstand the time travel length to get to the edges of the *EPL* borders."

He paused for a moment and the clock ticking got seemingly even louder.

Then he said firmly, "Earth needs us. Amazing as that may seem."

A shiver ran down her back and she took a deep breath, looking into the wonderful eyes of Brian Saber.

"I thought I was long past the point where anyone would ever need me."

"A few years ago," Brian said, "so did I."

They sat in silence for a moment, letting the clock tick on.

Finally she took a deep breath and realized just how tired she felt.

She slowly pushed her wheelchair back from his bed and turned it toward the door.

"Join me for Christmas breakfast?" she asked.

"I'd love to," he said, smiling. "And maybe soon we can go dancing again."

"Do you think that's possible? Really?"

"We're usually called for a mission at least once a week, if not more often," he said. "I think a dance or two just might be arranged."

"Thank you, Captain," she said. "For the best Christmas present anyone has ever given me. I will see you at breakfast."

"The pleasure will be all mine," he said.

She wheeled herself across the hall and to her bed.

A few moments later she was on her back, staring at the ceiling, remembering the feeling of standing, of walking without help, and of dancing.

Especially dancing.

She so loved to dance.

Tonight hadn't been a dream. She knew that now. She had fought aliens for the *Earth Protection League.*

She had danced with the most handsome man she had ever met.

And she would dance again.

For the first time in years, she actually had something to live for. Tomorrow at breakfast, she'd talk to Captain Brian Saber about all the wonders out there in the universe.

About her duties.

And what Earth needed from her.

It felt wonderful to be needed again, especially on Christmas.

She closed her eyes after a few minutes and drifted off to sleep.

And for the first night in a very long time, she didn't need to dream of dancing.

The Second Major Mission
Over Two Years Later

Nine

February 12th, 2021
Actual Earth Time
Location: Chicago

DOT WAS FEEDING Brian his applesauce one spoonful at a time when he saw their target.

Around them, the Shady Valley Nursing Home went on with its normal lunch routine, but today was going to be anything but normal. In fact, the survival of the human race might depend on what happened next.

He didn't want to think about the cost of failure. As the cliché often said, failure was not an option this time around.

The banging of dishes and the rumble of people talking made it almost impossible for Brian to be heard. So he and Dot had a signal for when he wanted her to stop with her feeding him his applesauce, about the only solid thing he could really eat these days. He didn't much mind, since the stroke had also taken his ability to taste anything.

And smell anything, and considering how little control he had of certain body functions since the stroke, he considered that a gift.

He blinked his right eye and she instantly pulled back, taking a napkin and wiping the drool from his chin.

Being eighty-eight was bad enough, but being mostly paralyzed from a series of strokes really sucked more than Brian could ever say. Thankfully Dorothy "Dot" Leeds made it bearable. And took care of him far more than she should. But she said she loved doing it and didn't mind in the slightest.

She was his best friend and had been for years before she had joined the *Earth Protection League*. Now they were in love, but both of them were slowly dancing around that topic.

The last stroke he had a year ago had taken most of his movement, but not his mind, and he could still speak, mostly softly.

He blinked twice, their signal for Dot to get close. She leaned in so she could hear his hoarse whisper over the noise of the others eating lunch, her wonderful, eighty-seven-year-old face still showing the signs of the beautiful younger woman he knew so well.

"What is it, Brian?" she asked.

She then turned her ear slightly so she could hear him clearly over the noise. They had had many great conversations in that very fashion.

"Doctor Jack Dalton, sitting at the second table over."

Her head snapped around to find Dalton.

Then she turned back to Brian, her eyes bright. "Heavy, brown, knitted sweater with the orange food stains?"

"Yes," Brian whispered.

He wished he could have nodded, but that wasn't possible anymore.

They both watched for a moment while Dalton struggled with a plate of food on a tray before he managed to get it arranged. His hands were twisted almost closed by years of arthritis, and they shook.

Brian had no idea how Dalton could even hold a spoon, but somehow he managed, which was a lot better than Brian could do.

Dalton's very thin gray hair didn't do anything to cover a mottled scalp, and his thick, gray eyebrows seemed more like large bugs on his wrinkled face than anything else.

That man, that ninety-one-year-old scientist, had to be on the mission with them in the next few hours. Or Earth and the entire *Earth Protection League* might not survive. That's what the generals had told them this morning.

Dot and Brian had been given the responsibility of recruiting Dalton. Brian had no idea how they were going to do that. Not a clue, short of just kidnapping him, with help from younger EPL service people, of course. He doubted he and Dot combined could kidnap a plate of food from the lunchroom without help and planning.

Brian knew that likely the mission would be a suicide mission. If Dr. Jack Dalton did come with them, there would be a high chance he would never return to Shady Valley Nursing Home.

Of course, if he didn't come and didn't help, there was a high chance that none of them would return.

And that Earth and Shady Valley Nursing Home might not even survive.

As Brian had always figured, it was better to die out in space fighting than sitting in a wheelchair with drool on his chin.

This mission would be no exception to that.

Ten

February 12th, 2021
Actual Earth Time
Location: Chicago

AFTER SEEING DALTON, Brian wasn't hungry, but Dot insisted on finishing feeding him, whispering to him that he had to have his strength up for the sex later on.

That made him blush. She liked when she could get the great Captain Brian Saber to blush.

Then she finished her lunch as well, and with some help from an orderly got Brian's wheelchair moved out into the hall where they could intercept Dalton when he came out of the lunchroom.

She could walk along behind his chair pushing it slowly, but getting him out of that cluster of tables and chairs of the lunchroom was always too much for her.

She stood, holding onto the back of Brian's chair, thinking and waiting.

This was so important, she had no idea how they were going to make it happen, and she was scared, more scared than she had been piloting any ship over the last few years.

They had to make this happen. They had no choice from what the general had told her in a rage call direct to her phone this morning. Never before had she been contacted by anyone from the EPL directly in her room.

Brian said that had only happened to him once as well, and they had almost lost Earth in that battle.

Brian's finger tapped the arm of his wheelchair and she looked up.

Dalton was using a cane as he slowly approached, his hand knotted around the top of the cane.

She stepped forward, holding onto Brian's chair but standing beside it.

"Doctor, my name is Dot Leeds and this is Brian Saber. Could we have a minute to talk to you?"

Dot had left off their Captain titles purposefully. She had become a captain of her own ship just over a year ago. She had made it to captain faster than even Brian had. But she had had Brian helping her.

Now, with Dalton, there was simply no point in making the guy think they were crazy right off. He was going to think that anyway in a few minutes as it was.

She remembered she thought Brian was crazy when he told her about the *Earth Protection League*.

"I'm not a medical doctor," Dalton said, slowly moving to go past them.

"I know that, Doctor Dalton," Dot said. "Until you wrote a paper on the subatomic connection between space and time and matter, you were considered one of the top physicists of all time. Maybe greater than Einstein."

That stopped him, so Dot kept going.

"Please, just a few minutes of your time?" Dot asked. "I know you are new here, just arrived last week, but there is something urgent we need to talk to you about."

She could tell that Brian wanted to give her some support, but the best he could do was a slight nod and even that was amazing. That stroke had taken so much from him a year ago.

Thankfully, what happened to this body here on Earth didn't affect him at all sixty years out in space.

Dalton stared at her for a moment, then at Brian. Finally, he nodded. "I guess I don't have much else to do."

Step one down. Dot could feel the relief.

Now came the hard part.

As Dot moved around behind Brian to push him behind Dalton, she noticed Brian managed to slide one finger over the edge of his chair and push a hidden button on his wheelchair signaling the *League* to stand ready.

Good. At least that much was done.

"In here," Dalton said, moving toward his room as they had figured he would do. He had a private room, as they all did. The *League* could be in his room within seconds when Dot gave Brian the signal to push the button again.

And Dalton's room had a somewhat sheltered sliding door to the interior garden, lawn, and patio area that the home surrounded. That would be the way they would all leave.

She knew for a fact she wouldn't be going back to her room today for her normal after-lunch nap. Both she and Brian would be doing a rare daytime extraction for this mission.

That's how important it was.

And if they didn't win this coming battle, she wouldn't be seeing her room ever again either.

Doctor Dalton went into his room and pulled a chair over, then got another one for Dot.

The room looked the same as the rest of the rooms, but Dalton had an old table surrounded by three chairs. He had some papers on the table and had clearly been working on something there.

Dot wheeled Brian to a position between the chairs, then using the bar on the end of Dalton's bed, she went back and closed the door, lowering the room into almost complete silence.

"So what's this all about?" Dalton asked. "And what could be so important that you would need to talk urgently with someone as old and discredited as I am?"

"Eventually your name will be honored," Dot said, smiling at Dalton as she sat beside Brian. "Because your theories are completely right. But you won't live to see it, I'm afraid."

He laughed. "What? Are they sending old people back from the future?"

Brian cleared his throat and then said as loudly as he could, "That's not how your theory works, is it, Doctor?"

Dot was impressed that Brian could talk that loudly.

Dalton again laughed. "No, it isn't."

"You suggested in your work," Dot said, "that time and matter and space are connected. Completely connected — not in the way most scientists believe, but in much deeper ways, correct?"

"Yes, so what?"

"You happen to be the right age," Brian said, "to help out humanity with that wonderful mind of yours, and maybe save us all."

He just stared at Brian and shook his head.

"Doctor, please listen to me all the way through," Dot said. "I am certain you will not believe me, but when I tell this story, please keep in mind your very own theory. Please? The story will only take a few minutes."

"I suppose my nap can wait that long," he said, shrugging.

Dot smiled.

She indicated Brian. "This is Captain Brian Saber, the most decorated ship's captain in all of the *Earth Protection*

League. My name is Captain Dorothy Leeds, but my friends call me Dot."

The Doctor started to speak, but Dot held up a hand to silence him. "The entire story first," she said.

"The *Earth Protection League* was formed back in a time long before Atlantis, when mankind first reached out into space. We were helped by other races we met in our local space neighborhood, and the *League* was formed and maintained even as mankind kept falling back into dark ages. Since governments don't last, no government knows about it."

"As years went by…" Brian said, his voice as clear as Dot had heard it in some time. Clearly he felt it critical that he help. He was always such a fighter. That was one of the many things she loved about him.

Brian took a deep breath and went on. "The EPL expanded its borders farther and farther out into space. The EPL now controls, with the help of many other races, a sphere sixty-plus light years around Earth."

"For centuries," Dot said, picking up the story, "everything was fine, until about ten years ago Earth-time. The *League* was suddenly attacked by what we call 'The Dogs,' an alien race bent on taking over and destroying Earth and all of Earth's allies."

Dalton started to say something, but Dot held up her hand and stopped him. Then she went on. "The Dogs were eventually beaten and pushed back to their borders, but not without a great loss of life on all the Earth bases out closer to the frontiers."

"So the *League* needed help," Brian said. "But because of your theory, it would be difficult to get help from Earth to the border quickly."

"They needed *old* help because of the very thing your theory described, Doctor," Dot said. "I don't really understand it, but it was explained to me that matter and time and space are permanently linked. So when a person climbs into a ship that can move through warped space, and thus get to a location great distances away quickly, the mass of the human body is still attached to its original space and time."

"In other words," Brian said, "I am eighty-eight sitting here. But if I go out sixty light-years using the Trans-Galactic Drive, I will arrive twenty-eight years old. And when I make the return voyage, arriving here within a half hour of when I leave, my body is again back to this state and age."

That amount of talking clearly tired Brian out. Dot could see that and she slipped his oxygen mask over his nose for a moment. He hated being in that old body. Just flat hated it. And she didn't blame him either.

"Over the centuries," Dot said, continuing the story that Dalton needed to hear, "scientists have managed to shelter the brain waves and thought patterns from the changes that happen as a body moves through great distances, so we keep our older minds in our younger bodies."

"You two are writing a book, aren't you? Some sort of science fiction book to make fun of my theories."

"We are not," Dot said, staring at Dalton. He was clearly angry and those bushy eyebrows were clutched together. "And they're *your* theories, Doctor. You proposed them; you had to know this would be an upshot of your theory if you were correct."

That shut the great physicist up completely.

The silence in the room seemed to crash in around them. Dot could hear her own heart beating and from what she could tell, Brian was breathing a little harder than normal.

Dalton leaned back, his old hands trembling, his face suddenly tired, but he was clearly thinking.

Finally, after a long moment of silence, he asked, "Why are you telling me this?"

"Because the *Earth Protection League* needs your help," Dot said. "Way beyond me to explain what they need you to do. Our job was to recruit you. And go with you. And have our ships run support for you."

"Into space?" Dalton asked.

"Into deep space," Dot said, nodding, keeping her intense gaze on the doctor. But as she did, she signaled to Brian with her right hand by pinching her fingers together.

It was time.

She could see out of the corner of her eye as Brian eased his finger toward the button that would call in the *League* to extract them. And then pushed it.

Dot took her gaze from Dalton and took off Brian's oxygen mask. In a moment he wouldn't need it.

"I'm not sure who is crazier," Dalton said, "you two, or me for listening to you."

"Isn't that what your critics said about you?" Brian asked, staring at the doctor. "Wouldn't you like to know, prove to yourself, that you were right?"

"You have no remaining family," Dot said, softly. "You are in this place until your last days. Alone. Trust me, going on missions is what Brian and I and our crews wait for, hold onto life for. Being young is wonderful. Being young with old, experienced minds, is even better. It makes living in a place like this worth the pain."

Dalton just sat there, saying nothing.

She and Brian had known that Dalton could never allow himself to agree. Just as both of them had never really said, "yes" to that first mission when they were recruited. It was just too crazy-sounding for any sane person to believe.

"We're going to prove this to you, Doctor," Brian said, as the sliding door leading out to the courtyard opened up and four young men and one woman walked in.

All were wearing civilian clothes, as was normal for extractions. But Dot knew all of them were Earth-bound members of the EPL. Or at least they would be Earth-bound until they got a lot older and could travel distances into space.

All five stopped and snapped off salutes to Brian and Dot.

Kennison, the young man who often carried Brian to the lift point, came over beside Brian, while the young woman named Sherri moved over beside Dot.

Dot stood.

She prided herself in walking to the extraction point, but it was always good to have an arm to hold onto.

The other three men flanked Doctor Dalton.

"It seems I have no choice but to play along with whatever this is," he said, standing slowly.

"You will believe us shortly," Dot said. "We'll talk again about sixty light-years from here."

With that Kennison picked Brian up like he didn't weigh anything.

Dot had to admit, the kid was gentle on Brian's old, thin skin, and Dot knew Brian appreciated that.

Kennison and Brian vanished just a step outside the door, leaving Doctor Dalton standing there, staring, with his mouth open. Usually, at night, they took them all the way to the center of the courtyard and used a tractor beam to lift them up. But it seemed, with a daylight extraction, the *League* was willing to take more chances.

"A form of teleportation," Dot said.

The doctor looked like he might have a heart attack before he got out of the room.

A moment later he and the three vanished just outside the door and then she let Sherri escort her out and pull the sliding door closed behind them before they were taken to the ship.

A moment later she was in the Trans-Galactic Drive transport ship in orbit and Sherri was lifting her and placing her gently into her sleep coffin.

Then she stepped back and snapped off a salute. "Have a safe voyage, Captain."

"Thanks," Dot said, giving a slight salute as the coffin lid closed over her.

She really, really hoped that she would see Sherri again. But that would only happen if she lived through the mission and they were successful.

And from what the general had hinted at on the phone this morning, that was doubtful.

Eleven

February 12th, 2061
Equivalent Earth Time
Location: Deep Space

BRIAN AWOKE AS usual to the faint, orange and rose smell of the sleep gas being flushed out of his sleep coffin. He reached up and pushed the lid open, relishing once again how wonderful it felt to actually be able to move his arms.

Move anything for that matter.

He sat up, and then levered himself out of the sleep coffin. He still had on his old clothes with the applesauce stains from breakfast, but he shed them quickly.

They did not smell good at all and he wrinkled his nose and tossed them into a cleaning bag to be washed while he was here. If he survived, the least he could do was have clean clothes going back.

He sometimes wondered how Dot put up with him in that old stroke-riddled body.

The room he awoke in wasn't his normal Captain's cabin on his own ship, *The Bad Business*. This looked more like a normal stateroom on a transport ship. All his clothes and gear were on a small dresser.

They usually transferred their sleep coffins to their cabins before they awoke anyone. That meant Dot was here on the transport as well, instead of in her cabin in her ship, *The Blooming Rose*.

He guessed they were going to talk to the doctor here, before heading out on the mission.

Brian quickly slipped on the black leather pants and white, pleated, silk shirt that was the standard Captain's uniform. He put on the black leather vest with the EPL logo on the front over his shirt, then buckled on the wide black-leather belt around his waist.

He sat down and pulled on the soft leather boots, tucking his pants legs loosely into the top of the tall boots. Then he took his two photon-blasters from the top of the dresser and put them in their holsters on his belt.

Captain Saber was back.

He stood and just stared in the mirror for a moment, just as he did with every mission, trying to make himself believe this was real, that the young Saber was standing there, not the old, stroke-damaged Saber who lived on Earth and couldn't move.

He hoped at some point to ask Dot to marry him and file for permission to settle down on a planet out here on the frontier, maybe even have some kids and work on growing old once again, doing only local missions. That was his plan, but right now he and Dot were taking it slow. They both had previous spouses they both had loved. It felt odd to be starting over again at such an advanced age.

But he loved her. At some point he would get the courage to ask her to marry him. The rules were that you could only settle out here on the edge of the *EPL* if you were married, except for rare cases.

But right now, instead of thinking about marrying Dot, he had another mission to complete if he had any hope of ever having that happen.

He opened the stateroom door and headed down the hallway toward the ship's lounge. That's where the crew would take the doctor when they woke him.

As he turned the corner, Brian saw Dot striding toward him, dressed as he was, but with only one Photon Blaster on her hip.

She was the most beautiful woman he had ever seen. Her wonderful brown hair was pulled back and her smile filled the corridor. She never once failed in taking his breath away.

"Hi, handsome," she said, kissing him firmly.

He kissed her back, not wanting to let her go.

Finally she laughed. "I told you that applesauce would get you going."

"Trust me," he said, "it's not the applesauce."

With that, they both laughed and turned and went into the lounge.

Doctor Dalton stood near the huge window that looked out over the fleet of ships surrounding the transport ship. From the number, it looked like the League was expecting all sorts of trouble on this mission.

The *EPL* ships looked more like a large flock of birds floating there in space than anything. Even to Brian they looked impressive.

Brian dismissed the guard standing beside the door and he and Dot moved over toward the doctor, through the tables and chairs that filled the lounge area around a small dance floor. He and Dot had spent many a fun evening in this lounge and on that dance floor before returning to Earth.

Dancing was something he loved to remember when trapped in that old body.

Dot loved it more than he did.

The doctor was standing with his left hand pressed flat against the window, staring around his hand at all the stars.

He looked just like a younger version of the man in the nursing home, only his hair was thick and his face much smoother. He still had the extremely thick eyebrows. And, of course, his hands were clearly healthy, something that seemed to be amazing him even more than the space and the fleet of ships.

He just kept pushing his hand flat against the view port, then looking at it.

"Doctor," Brian said. "I'm Captain Saber. This is Captain Leeds."

Dalton turned and looked at them, then just shook his head. "The two from the nursing home? How is that possible? How is any of this possible?"

"Yes, sir," Dot said. "It's possible because your theories are correct."

He stared at his hand as he opened and closed it.

He and Dot stood there silently, letting the great mind inside that head fight to grasp the evidence in front of him.

Then Dalton looked up at them. "I was right? I actually was right?"

"You were, sir," Brian said, nodding. "We are sixty light years from Earth. You are in your thirty-one-year-old body, the exact same body you had sixty years ago."

He pulled up the clean white shirt the service had supplied him and stared at the scar on his stomach. "Even my appendix is still gone. Lost that when I was twenty-seven."

"If we had gone four more light years out," Brian said, "you would still have it."

Dalton nodded, then turned again and put his hand on the window, pushing it flat, something he clearly couldn't do in his old body back on Earth.

After a moment, he turned back and looked at Brian. "Captain Saber, there was a reason you and Captain Leeds didn't let me live out my last days not knowing the truth. And I'm sure it was not simply a gesture of kindness. So what can I do for the *League*, as you call it, to earn my keep?"

Brian smiled, glad that the doctor had come around so quickly.

"I honestly don't know for sure," Brian said. "I will let the *League* scientists brief you. However I do know that our enemy, the Dogs, have somehow designed some sort of major weapon that

"The two from the nursing home? How is that possible? How is any of this possible?"

has the chance of disconnecting time and space and matter."

He thought for a moment, finally shaking his head. "I can't imagine how that would be possible, now that I know my theory was correct. But I also don't understand how it could be used as a weapon."

Brian pointed at the fleet as Dot told him the answer.

"Almost all of the crews of all those battleships are senior citizens from Earth, just as the three of us are. It was the only choice the *League* had to get recruits quickly after we lost so many in that first war with the Dogs."

The doctor nodded. "Sever the connection, and we end up back on Earth, in our old bodies."

"And the frontier of the *Earth Protection League*," Brian said, "all the *League*, actually, will be undermanned and outgunned. All these warships would be suddenly empty. The *League* would fall."

Dalton nodded, giving one last look at the ships floating outside the big window.

"Where are the *Earth Protection League* scientists? I will need to get caught up quickly if I am to help."

Brian pointed at the largest ship in the center of the fleet. "They are on the admiral's ship, the *Tuesday Morning*.

"Can you take me there?" Dalton asked, again seeming to get lost in the fantastic view of ships and stars.

"You'll be taken there," Brian said. "Captain Leeds and I have our own ships to get ready for this coming fight."

"Thank you," Dalton said, again staring at his healthy hand, flexing it. "I'll try to repay this kindness."

"Just save us all, Doc," Brian said.

With that the three of them turned and left the lounge, stopping in the hallway outside.

With a wink to Dot, Brian signaled they were ready for transport, and a moment later he was in the hallway of his ship, *The Bad Business*, headed for the bridge.

If he had anything to say about it, he and Dot and the doctor would be enjoying drinks and dancing in that lounge very soon, celebrating their victory.

Chapter Twelve

February 12th, 2061
Equivalent Earth Time
Location: Deep Space

BRIAN STROLLED INTO the Command Center of *The Bad Business* and dropped in to the big center chair facing a wall of screens. The Command Center was actually fairly small, with only four stations. Usually his second-in-command, Marian Knudson, a stunning redhead from Wisconsin, sat in the chair to his left, but this time she had moved over to the communications chair directly behind him. Just from what little he knew so far of this mission, he needed someone he could trust at the communications station, especially since he had a hunch they were going over the border.

Marian knew that and had already moved.

Carl Turner, the best navigator in the fleet was in the chair to his right.

"So what's happening, Captain?" Carl asked, his boyish face turning to look up at him. Brian could see that Carl was worried, not an emotion he normally showed in any way.

Carl appeared to be in his teens and had a face full of freckles. This far out, Carl was actually only twenty-one. Brian was twenty-eight or so. Carl was the youngest member of his crew, but Dot had a few slightly younger on her crew.

"From the best I can figure," Brian said, "and what little information I've been given, we're going to be getting a little younger. We have to take the fight to the Dogs."

"I hope I don't have to fly this thing in diapers," Carl said, shaking his head and turning back to his screens that surround his chair.

"We all hope that," Marian said from behind Brian.

Suddenly, across all the dozens of screens in the command center, an image of the area of space they were in came up. Admiral Lincoln's voice boomed out of the speaker, and Marian at the communications panel moved quickly to dampen it a little as Brian studied the three-dimensional chart on the big screen in front of him.

"Make sure everyone on the ship is getting this," Brian said to Marian and she nodded.

"The Dogs are on the verge of creating a new weapon," the admiral said over the image, "that will disconnect us all from this time and area of space and send us home."

Brian knew that much.

"They are within hours of launching the new weapon over the border and sending it toward Earth, followed by their fleet."

"Hours?" Carl said softly, then whistled under his breath.

Brian agreed with that shock. No wonder the brass had been in a hurry to extract everyone and get everyone staged. Brian had no idea there was so little time.

The screen showed the location of the EPL fleet, and then the location across the line that divided EPL space from Dog space. The weapon seemed to be on a big moon in a system three light years beyond the border.

"We're going to get five years younger if we go in there," Carl said, doing the quick math. "I'm going to have pimples again. Damn."

The illustration also showed a large fleet of Dog ships staging about four light years on the other side of the moon's system.

Brian didn't like the looks of that at all. EPL warships were far more powerful than Dog warships and had beat Dog ships before numbers of times. But EPL just didn't have enough ships out here on the edge to take on that entire fleet at once.

Not good, not good at all.

The admiral went on, not showing himself but instead just talking over the image of the ships and the moon with the weapon. "If we jump in and catch them by surprise, we'll only be outgunned about three-to-one around the weapon. But that Dog fleet will be coming in fast, so we won't have more than fifteen minutes at most."

"Ten," Brian said.

"Nine," Carl said.

Brian trusted Carl more than he trusted either the admiral or his own rough calculations.

"My first desire is to destroy everything on that moon," the admiral said,

"including the weapon, but my science advisors warn me that if the weapon is functioning, that might set off a cascade effect. So we are going to let the science boys work on the problem of destroying the weapon for one more hour. Stand by at my command to jump in one hour."

At that his voice cut off, but the image of the border, the big moon, and the Dog fleet remained.

"I sure hope the guest we brought can come up with something," Brian said, staring at the impossible fight that they faced.

"Who's the guest?"

"Dr. Jack Dalton," Brian said.

Carl laughed. "This ought to be messing with his brain. Didn't he get discredited for even suggesting that all this is possible in physics?"

"He did," Brian said.

"Let's hope he's not bitter," Marian said.

Chapter Thirteen

February 12th, 2061
Equivalent Earth Time
Location: Deep Space

BRIAN SAT FOR the next forty-five minutes in his big command chair, not moving. There was just nothing he could do. Beside him Carl ran over calculations and in the fourth station Marian made sure all the ships were in close contact so they could work together when the fighting started.

Mostly Brian just stared at the area of battle and the space between here and there. He knew for a fact that the Dogs were watching the EPL fleet just as carefully.

At one point, two more of EPL warships appeared as late reinforcements.

Brian had no doubt that if every ship in the EPL fleet prepared to jump, the Dog fleet would do the same, and they would have even less time than the nine minutes Carl thought they all might have.

Brian slowly came to the conclusion that jumping the entire fleet at that moon just wouldn't work.

Suddenly, he knew what had to be done. "Marian, put me through to a private line with the admiral."

She smiled. "We're going in alone, aren't we?"

"Well, that would figure," Carl said. "Sounds like us."

Brian laughed, not wanting to tell her that she had guessed correctly. "Just put me through."

The admiral came on and said, "Yes, Captain."

The admiral clearly lived out here in this area of space, since his face was wrinkled and he showed his age. He hadn't come in from Earth. Brian had met him a few times after missions and never really had gotten a read on the admiral's age.

He had on full uniform, including his admiral's hat that looked more like a kid's hat with a long point, only made out of pure white cloth like the admiral's uniform. The hat actually looked almost silly.

"Has Doctor Dalton come up with anything yet?" Brian asked.

The admiral glanced over his shoulder, then turned back to the screen. "He believes a concentrated Electro-Magnetic-Pulse would shut the thing down safely and then conventional weapons could destroy it."

"If it's running, how close can we get?"

The admiral leaned forward and punched a board in front of him, showing the big moon. It took Brian a moment to see what the admiral was showing him.

"All the Dog ships are standing off, away from the planet," Brian said. "The thing is running."

"It would seem so," the admiral said, nodding, a grim look on his wrinkled face.

Brian nodded, then explained his plan and his reasons for it to the admiral.

"That will buy you all time back here," Brian said, "to rig up larger EMP weapons to stop it from a safe distance."

"Doctor Dalton believes the effects of the device will cover a sphere of two light years when launched and fully powered."

Now Brian was confused again. "Where is it going to get that kind of power?"

The admiral leaned back, then said abruptly, "I don't know. I'll be right back with you."

Beside Brian, Carl's fingers were moving at lightning speed over his board as the admiral's wrinkled old face was again replaced by the map.

"No sub-atomic reaction can produce that kind of energy," Carl said, "since the field it's generating would shut it down."

"They are using the moon as a spaceship," Brian said. "How big is that moon?"

"It's actually about the size of Earth's moon," Carl said.

"They are going to move something the size of the moon *and* power that weapon at the same time?" Brian asked. "That makes no sense without the very process they are shutting down."

Suddenly Carl and Brian looked at each other, smiling.

"They have a shield that protects their own power sources," Brian said.

"Which means, given time, we can develop shields as well," Carl said, smiling. "We just need to buy them time somehow."

"Exactly what I was thinking," Brian said, smiling at Carl.

Brian again signaled that Marian punch in a call to the admiral. As his face appeared, Brian said, "They have shields protecting their power sources."

"That's what Doctor Dalton just told me," the admiral said, smiling. "Can you buy us some time?"

"We are thinking exactly the same, Admiral. I'll be ready in ten minutes. Could you have Dalton send over targeting and frequency levels of the needed EMP blast?"

"I'll do one better. He'll join you in two minutes. And I'm sending *The Blooming Rose* with you. You'll run the first wave, she'll target with conventional weapons once you shut the thing down."

"Yes, sir," Brian said.

It always worried Brian when Dot went into any battle, but he had learned to click off the worry and just trust her. And it only took him a second to do that again.

He turned to Carl as the admiral's face vanished from the screen again. "Can we focus an EMP wave tight enough to target that weapon?"

""I'll have it ready in five," Carl said, his fingers again flying over the board.

Brian watched, amazed. He knew for a fact that Carl had lost both hands and one leg at seventy in a car wreck. Yet there he was moving so fast his fingers looked like a blur. It had to be really hard for him to go back to Earth after each mission, but never once had Brian heard Carl complain.

A moment later, Dr. Dalton appeared standing behind Carl, looking sort of stunned at the sudden change of location.

"They need to put a tingle or a noise on that transporter, don't they?" Brian said, standing and shaking the doctor's hand. "Great work."

"The other scientists did most of it," he said as Brian had him sit down in Marian's normal chair to Brian's left.

Brian introduced him to Carl and Marian, then Carl and Dalton quickly got to work on the calculations for the EMP blast.

"That's powerful enough to shut just about anything down in that weapon," the doctor said, nodding, "even if shielded from most EMP blasts. And that sudden shutdown will collapse the building sub-atomic field of the weapon."

"And if it *doesn't* shut it down and we bomb the thing?" Brian asked.

"With luck, nothing," Dalton said. "But it also might send a cascade wave through the area, in a radius of about ten light years. I suggested to the admiral that just as we are about to attack the weapon he move his fleet back four or five light years."

"Good idea," Brian said.

"Captain Leeds," Marian said, as Dot's face filled the screen in front of Brian.

"Captain," Brian said.

Dot smiled. "Captain. Are you ready?"

Brian glanced at Carl, and then at the doctor.

Both nodded.

"Give the machine five seconds to shut down," Dalton said.

Dot nodded that she had heard. "We'll be exactly seven seconds behind you, on the same path. "Don't go stopping suddenly or we all might be in for a mess."

He laughed. "See you on the dance floor."

She smiled. "I don't know. My dance card is pretty full."

With that she clicked off.

That had been their ritual since their first night together dancing. So far it had pulled them through a lot of tight scrapes.

Brian clicked on the com link to the ship. "Be prepared to lay down covering fire for *The Blooming Rose* coming in behind us on my command. Stand by for jump."

Carl nodded. "Course plotted and in. You have exactly five seconds to fire after we appear near the weapon. We're going to be appearing right on the edge of those Dog warships standing off a distance from the weapon just to make sure we're not affected by it, either."

"So all hell is going to break loose," Brian said, nodding.

"With luck, we'll catch them by surprise," Carl said.

Marian's voice over the com-link counted down from five.

Five very, very long seconds.

"Engage," Marian said.

Carl's fingers flew over the panel and Brian took control of his ship.

A moment later they were five years farther out from Earth, and five years younger than they had been a moment before.

Around them was a small fleet of Dog warships, scattered in their standard, bowling-pin order, clearly just waiting to move.

Brian targeted the large area that was the weapon on the planet below, focusing down on the very center.

"Up the frequency ten percent," Dalton said, staring at the readings on the screen in front of him. "It's larger than we had calculated.

Carl's fingers flew, and an instant later he said, "Done."

Brian fired.

The invisible EMP blast hit the weapon base without any sort of impact.

Usually when Brian fired at something, things exploded. Not this time, but he kept firing anyway.

He could see that the Dog ships were turning, moving to attack. But it was taking them seconds, so they had been caught by surprise.

Dr. Dalton said, "The weapon is shutting down."

At that moment, a Dog warship opened fire, rocking the entire ship with two solid hits.

"Screens holding!" Carl said.

"Return fire!" Brian ordered over the shipboard com link.

He kept *The Bad Business* moving ahead as right behind them Dot's ship appeared and instantly started blasting the base. Her shots made an instant and clearly seen impact as the entire base started to shudder and explode.

"Covering fire for *The Blooming Rose*," Brian ordered all gunners.

Dot ignored all the fire she was taking from the Dogs, as all of her weapons were trained on the planet's surface.

"Our screens at sixty percent," Carl reported as more hits rocked them.

He kept his focus on the base below, holding the intense EMP blast on the weapon on the moon's surface.

"Blooming Rose's screens are at forty-two percent and holding," Carl reported, his voice calm.

Brian didn't know how long Dot's ship could hold out, but his gunners were doing a fantastic job of blowing up the closest Dog ships, creating a shield of exploding Dog ships for *The Blooming Rose*.

"Weapon is shut down," Dalton said, excitement clearly filling his voice.

Brian cut off the EMP blast and moved his ship closer to Dot's to help in the fight.

A moment later Dot stopped firing at the planet and began firing at the attacking ships. Brian could see from the readouts that *The Blooming Rose* had taken some damage, but Dot's screens were still holding.

"*The Blooming Rose* has done it," Carl said.

Brian snapped open a link to Dot.

"Let's go dancing," Brian said as her smiling face appeared.

A moment later, Carl jumped them out of the fight.

Brian just hoped Carl had jumped them in the right direction. He didn't think he could get much younger and he knew Carl couldn't.

They appeared right beside the EPL fleet at the point where the fleet had retreated in case the weapon had exploded.

A moment later *The Blooming Rose* appeared as well.

And Brian let out the breath he was holding.

On the view screen showing the Dogs' weapon moon, a fireworks display was happening; then after a moment, the Dog ships close to the planet jumped back to their own fleet.

And a few seconds later the moon exploded, looking like a small nova going off.

Wow, there had been a lot of energy on that planet.

"Are we safe, Doc?" Carl asked.

Doctor Dalton nodded, staring at the screen in front of him. "We are far enough away to not be bothered by that."

Brian glanced at Carl, then turned to the doctor. "So it worked?"

Dalton was still studying the readouts on the station in front of him, his thick eyebrows moving up and down as if they had a life of their own.

After a long moment, he turned and smiled, his huge eyebrows now up at the edge of his hairline. "It worked perfectly. I don't know about you, but I haven't felt this good in years."

"Yeah, space travel will do that for you," Carl said.

Chapter Fourteen

February 12th, 2061
Equivalent Earth Time
Location: Deep Space

DOT AND BRIAN came off the dance floor in the center of the large meeting room on the admiral's ship, laughing and both out of breath. Around them the dancers kept going, and the laughter filled the room louder than most parties.

The smells of the tables full of food against one wall still filled the air with ham and fresh bread. Not only had she danced too much, she had eaten too much, and maybe had a few too many drinks.

Everyone was happy tonight. And drinking.

She just felt happy to be alive. And with Brian.

Dot fanned herself, leaning against Brian. Even young, those fast songs of the 1950s and 1960s were work. She liked the slower ones. She had many very fond memories of slow dances from the earlier times, and with Brian in the last few years.

She still couldn't believe she could dance again. It was all such a dream at times.

They dropped down into chairs next to Dr. Dalton, who had just finished a conversation with Admiral Lincoln, who nodded to them as he left.

Dalton was smiling wider than she had ever seen a man smile before.

"So what's the great news?" Brian asked.

"Too much to believe," Dalton said, his smile getting ever bigger.

"You got to tell us before you explode," Dot said, laughing. It was a lot of fun to see a person so full of pure joy.

Dalton nodded and took a deep breath and then said quickly, "The admiral just got word from the *League* authorities that I will be allowed special permission, even though I am not married, to stay out here and continue my work as a young man again."

He said it so fast, he clearly couldn't believe it was true.

Dalton again opened and closed his hand, staring at it, clearly still stunned that he could do such a simple movement once again.

"Fantastic news," Doctor, Brian said.

"Wonderful, Doctor," Dot said, patting his arm. "The *EPL* needs you to help develop those screens."

"The admiral said I could continue my own work as well," Dalton said.

Dot smiled. She wondered what other fantastic things he would come up with, now that he had the freedom.

And the time.

And the belief in himself again.

"I have some applesauce to wear off," Brian said, smiling at Dot and pulling her to her feet.

She laughed at the impish grin on his handsome, young face, as a slow song started.

One thing about being young again with an old mind, you treasured every moment and every dance.

Right now, after escaping death once again, she wanted to treasure far more dances with the man of her dreams before she returned to that old body.

The Third Major Mission
Six Months Later

Chapter Fifteen

September 3rd, 2021
Actual Earth Time
Location: Chicago

THE YOUNG, STRONG Lieutenant Kennison gently nudged Captain Brian Saber in his nursing home bed, pulled back the light brown blanket and sheet covering him, and then easily picked Brian up with strong arms.

Brian was going on a mission.

Brian could feel the excitement surge through his old body yet again.

A mission, a chance to live again, to be young again.

He made himself take as deep a breath as he could without setting off a fit of coughing. His stroke-crippled body just couldn't take much at this point, but the promise of a mission always got him excited.

The Shady Valley Nursing Home room hadn't changed since Brian fell asleep at 10 p.m. Now his old clock on the wall told him it was a little after one in the morning. If he survived this mission, he would be back in fifteen minutes. But he might be out there in space for a month or more, if he was lucky.

The young lieutenant turned for the room's sliding glass door. Behind him Brian caught a glimpse of Captain Dorothy "Dot" Leeds being carried from her room across the hall and into his room by Lieutenant Sherri.

She followed Brian and Lieutenant Kennison out into the night air of a Chicago late summer night. The air was thick and heavy and the smell of freshly mowed grass surprised him.

The light nightshirt Brian wore to bed was almost too much for the warm night. He used to love being out in nights like this when he was younger and married. Now it made it hard for him to breathe, but he wouldn't be out in the humid, thick air long enough for it to matter.

Overhead, he could see the full moon, bright in the night sky. He and Dot were both far too old to ever walk under that moon, even on a warm night. But at some point in the near future, he hoped they would be together, staring up at some moon, somewhere in this sector of space.

No one talked.

He could hardly speak anymore, but none of the other three bothered either. It was all business for all of them.

They were on a mission.

Around the country right now his crew, and Dot's crew, were going through the same routine.

Damn he was excited.

He always felt this way going on a mission.

The four of them neared the center of the courtyard of the nursing home. He could feel the humidity forming slight sweat on his face and neck, but there was nothing he could do to wipe it away.

The full moon was so beautiful on a clear summer night. He hoped he would see it again later.

Then a yellow beam struck them from above and lifted all four of them up easily into the big intergalactic transport ship.

The cooler, thinner air of the ship covered him and behind him he heard Dot say softly, "See you on the other side."

He would have answered her, but he couldn't talk louder than a whisper at a good moment. He couldn't walk or even lift his arms at all either. A stroke a little over a year ago had taken most of those skills.

She knew that and didn't expect an answer from him.

They were both very much in love.

At some point soon he hoped to ask her to marry him and live out on the frontier, not ever having to return to earth and their old bodies. He hadn't gotten around to it yet, but hoped to very soon.

She hadn't brought it up either, but he knew she was just old-fashioned enough to not do that. And since they hadn't talked about it, he wasn't sure if she understood the rules of living out at the edge of the *EPL* space. They really needed to talk about it.

And he needed to flat ask her to marry him.

But right now they were still frontline fighters. And clearly they were needed.

Lieutenant Kennison put Brian down in his sleep coffin in a private cabin off to one side of the big hallway and stepped back and snapped off a salute. "Good luck, sir," he said.

Then he lowered the lid until it latched over Brian and the light went out.

Brian would have loved to salute the young man back, but he couldn't. He couldn't even wipe off the drip of sweat threatening to run into his right eye.

Instead, he just lay there thinking of seeing Dot again in her young and youthful body.

And he thought of them dancing as they always did after a mission.

But first they had to survive whatever faced them in deep space this time.

A faint orange and rose smell seeped into the coffin and Captain Brian Saber dozed off.

Chapter Sixteen

September 3rd, 2021
Equivalent Earth Time
Location: Deep Space

BRIAN AWOKE WHAT seemed like just an instant later.

He reached up and easily pushed the coffin lid open. Then he levered his young body out of the sleep chamber.

He never got tired of that feeling after being trapped in that wheelchair and bed what seemed like just moments before. The magic of the Trans-Galactic speed had done it to him again, given him his young body back.

He had sure taken this body for granted when he had been young. He didn't now. Not for a moment.

The memory of his stroke-beaten body was always just too fresh in his mind when he was in this younger body.

He quickly slipped off the old nightshirt and tossed it back in the coffin. He would need that for the return trip back.

If he survived.

He pushed that thought away.

If he didn't, his son would be called in the middle of the night and there would be a funeral for a body that looked like his old body that was a fake. And no one but those in the *Earth Protection League* would know Brian Saber of Chicago died in space, fighting for the safety of all humanity.

And Brian didn't honestly care if anyone knew. He just loved doing this, getting a chance to be young again.

This trip they must have gone a little farther out in distance from Earth. He looked to be about twenty-five. Often he ended up closer to thirty on missions.

So that meant they were very, very close to the *EPL* border, more than likely the border with the Dogs.

He quickly dressed, then with one last look in the mirror as he always did, he left his room, turning right and heading for the command center.

He was on his own warship, *The Bad Business.*

Dot would have been transferred to her ship as well, *The Blooming Rose*. He wished he could see her now, kiss her, hold her with his young strong arms. But there would be time for that later.

Right now he had to focus on the mission they faced, whatever it was.

He got to the Command Center just a few seconds before his other two command crew arrived.

Marian Knudson, took her second chair to his left and started working on the boards in front of her, bringing up the screens in the command center to show the area of space they were in. The two of them had been a team for years now.

She was tough, all business, and smart as they came.

This time she had her red hair long and down over her shoulders. Usually she kept it up tight against her head.

Behind them Carl dropped into his chair with a "Damn this feels good. Home again."

Brian felt the same way.

The small command center with its four chairs and many screens and control boards was his home.

"I like my home on Earth," Marian said.

Back in Wisconsin, Marian lived alone, even at the age of ninety, in her own home. As Carl had said once, she was too damn mean to die or live anywhere else.

Marian had not argued with that, only smiled that smile that let Brian know that at some point Carl would pay for the remark.

"So any news as to the mission, Captain?" Marian asked, her fingers running over the board in front of her. "We are within striking distance of the Dog border. Much closer than normal, actually, which is why Carl here has pimples. No sign at all of Dog warships."

"There are six other EPL ships with us," Carl said. "One is *The Blooming Rose*."

Everyone knew about his and Dot's relationship. They had made no attempt at all to keep it a secret. There had been no point and no one had seemed to care.

"No word yet," Brian said. "But I suspect we don't have long to wait."

He pointed to the board in front of him, and as he did, a red light started blinking, meaning an emergency message was coming in.

"You creep me out every time you do that," Carl said, shaking his head and turning back to his board.

Brian just smiled at Marian. The brass had a certain timetable that they allowed the crews to get into positions on their ships, and that timetable never varied, so Brian always knew when the message was coming in.

"Message on screen," Carl said a moment later.

General Holmes's face appeared, his frown causing his middle-aged face to wrinkle even more than it already was. His hair was balding and he looked like he had recently seen too much sun on that exposed skin.

They had worked a few times with General Holmes. He was in charge of the defense forces in the ground bases scattered along the EPL borders.

"Captains," he said, nodding. "I'm afraid this is as bad as it gets."

Brian said nothing, as did the other captains of the other six warships, so the general went on.

"The Dogs have launched a moon at Earth."

Brian sat there hoping that General Holmes would take back that statement.

He didn't.

The general just kept frowning.

"The moon is accelerating from deep in Dog space and will be at the border at your position in about six hours."

"Fleet of ships with it I assume?" Saber asked.

The general shook his head. "They don't think they need ships on this one. The moon they have launched is as big as our moon around Earth. It's not carrying a weapon like they tried last time. The moon is the weapon."

Brian sat back and tried to imagine what it would take to get a moon like that actually moving, what kind of power and how the moon would even hold together. And how they would even aim it from such a long distance through space.

And how many thousands of years at real-space travel it would take to get to Earth.

"I'm sending all the data we have on it through to all of you," the general said. "We want you to investigate the moon the moment it crosses into our space, pass on the data to our scientists on bases closer to Earth."

With that he clicked off, leaving the screen blank.

"Why do I think there's something he flat omitted from that briefing," Carl said.

Marian's fingers flew over her board as Brian sat there, waiting. He knew Carl was right. The General wasn't telling them everything. There was something more.

"Oh, shit," Marian said.

Brian looked over at her. She never swore.

She put up the report that made her swear on the main screen in front of Brian so that they could all see it.

"One hour after the moon crosses into our space," Marian said, "it reaches Trans-Galactic speed and will be protected by the Trans-Galactic shields. Nothing will be able to change its course until it plows into Earth."

"They built a T-G drive big enough to power a moon at full speed," Carl said, shaking his head. "Wow! That's impressive. So how about we just stop it like we did the last time they tried to launch a moon?"

Brian had to admit, it was impressive. But there was only one problem. Once something was in Trans-Galactic drive, it couldn't be stopped. It wasn't in real time and the shields that formed with the drive could plow through anything.

So they had to figure out a way to stop a speeding moon before it got up to speed completely.

Or Earth would be destroyed very, very shortly.

Chapter Seventeen

September 3rd, 2021
Equivalent Earth Time
Location: Deep Space

BRIAN LOOKED AROUND at his command crew, then shook his head. "Looks like we got seven hours to figure this out. Marian, make sure to get that report to everyone on board who understand Trans-Galactic drive physics."

Marian nodded, her fingers moving quickly over the controls as Brian swiveled his big chair completely around so he could see Carl on his right and Marian on his left in the small command center.

Actually he was facing the door, but since his chair was slightly ahead of theirs at point in the room, they could all talk this way. His back was to his screens, but they could still access their screens while they talked.

"Done," she said.

Brian knew that meant the other thirty-some members of his crew all knew the score and were working on solutions as well. When you had that many experienced people working hard on something, results tended to happen.

And Brian knew that everyone on the other ships were doing the same. That was a lot of years experience focused on the same problem. One of the advantages of having a lot of really old minds in young bodies.

"Let me kind of think out loud here," Brian said.

Both Marian and Carl nodded.

"I assume T-G space will power the thing once the moon reaches hyperspace speed. But what's powering it now?"

Both Carl and Marian had the report at their fingertips and it was Marian who spoke first. "The moon has a hot core, so the engines spaced around the moon are feeding off the internal core of the moon itself."

"All T-G engines," Carl said. "Are shielded from EMP blasts as would be expected since we toasted their last moon. Nothing we have will knock them out."

Brian knew that and he nodded. He'd been in a lot of fights with Dog warships and knocking their engines out was never an option, just as Dogs knocking out a T-G *EPL* engine wasn't possible either. It was the nature of Trans-Galactic engines and the force fields that built up around them.

"Can we dig the engines out of the moon's surface outside the shields?" Brian asked.

Again both his command crew worked on the report, then both shook their heads at the exact same time. "Engines are buried thirty miles deep inside the moon. No dislodging them."

Brian looked at the big screen near Carl with the report and wondered how the *EPL* got all the information. More than likely a number of good people had died for it.

"And I assume no blowing the moon apart before it enters Trans-Galactic speed?" Brian asked.

"They found the most stable hunk of rock I've ever seen," Carl said and Marian nodded.

"It would take an entire fleet of ships," Carl said, sounding disgusted, "pounding it with all weapons, and I doubt that even that much would make more than a dent."

They all three sat there in silence. Brian just kept looking around, looking at his young body, at his command crew's young bodies. Somehow they had made it out here, to this exact location in space.

And suddenly he knew that was the key to this.

He looked at Carl. "Who is driving the moon?"

"No one will be on the moon," Carl said, looking at the report.

"So who drives us when we come out here," Brian asked. "Who gets us to exact coordinates, with Trans-Galactic drives, in those transport ships."

Marian frowned and turned back to her board.

Carl did the same thing.

Brian knew he was on to something and something important. You don't just send a ship hurtling through more miles of space than Brian wanted to think about without something or someone driving. Even with top shields, you didn't want to plow holes through things along the way that didn't need holes in them.

So those transport ships from Earth had someone driving it, controlling it, from somewhere.

And that moon would have someone driving all the way to Earth. One planet that far away was far, far too small a target to hit from over sixty light years of distance without a number of course corrections along the way.

"Computers," Marian finally said. "Each transport we take out here is run by a computer to do course corrections."

"Through sensors, the computer is able to see the route ahead," Carl said, "and make corrections to avoid the transport putting a hole in something else along the way."

"So there is a computer on that moon somewhere?" Brian asked. "We know where?"

"Buried with the Trans-Galactic drive engines," Marian said quickly.

"Damn," Carl said, clearly getting angry. "They thought of everything."

"Not everything," Brian said, smiling. "Is the moon rotating in any fashion?"

Carl and Marian both looked puzzled at him, then quickly checked.

"No," Marian said. "It couldn't rotate and maintain its T-G drive thrust."

"So we blind it," Brian said. "Tough to hit anything without being able to see."

"The computer sensors," Carl said, laughing. "Of course, they would have to be hidden on the front side of the moon to feed the computer."

"And I'll wager those sensors are not hardwired into that computer," Brian said. "Not through that much rock."

Marian laughed, the first time Brian had heard that for some time. "What are you thinking, Captain?"

"We going to just blow those sensors off the face of the moon?" Carl asked.

Brian sat back, his hands behind his head, smiling. "I have a better idea."

"Oh, I love it when he smiles like that," Carl said, laughing.

"How about," Brian said, "we feed those computers in that moon some bad targeting information, something simple such as the location of a big Dog military base."

"Oh, that will annoy them something awful," Carl said, laughing so hard tears were coming to his eyes.

Marian informed all the other ships of the idea and then all three of them set to work on exactly where on that moon those sensors would be planted and how to intercept the signal from the surface sensors to the moon targeting computer.

The fallback plan was to wipe all the sensors from the face of the moon and hope it missed Earth. But Brian liked his plan a lot better, and didn't let that moon even get into *EPL* space.

Chapter Eighteen

September 3rd, 2021
Equivalent Earth Time
Location: Deep Space

THE MOON WAS fast approaching the *EPL* border when *Earth Protection League* Command gave the clearance to try their plan. It had been a scientist on Dot's ship who had finally cracked the Dog computer code between the moon targeting computer and the sensors.

And it had been a scientist on yet another warship who had figured out how to intercept the signals from the sensors.

They needed to have a ship in tight over each of the six sensors on the moon and the intercept would have to be sent at exactly the same moment to all sensors.

In essence, the control of the moon was going to be transferred to Brian. He and Carl and Marian were going to turn the moon just before it started into Trans-Galactic drive and fire it at a Dog military base.

And then destroy the targeting computer with a very nasty virus.

That moon would wipe out that Dog base and then head out into deep space at full T-G drive. The engines would have to fail before that moon dropped back into normal space a very, very long ways away from this entire galaxy.

At least that was the plan.

But there was one major problem with the plan that Brian didn't much like.

Six *EPL* ships would have to basically hover in close over the moon to intercept the signal from each sensor and relay the signal to his ship and then, in turn, take the new instructions and feed them back into the sensors.

Dot and her ship would be one of those in close. They would have to stay in close during the moon's turn and then somehow get a safe distance away when the moon jumped to Trans-Galactic Drive.

It was going to take exact timing. Just a second or two of delay and a warship would be lost.

And if one warship didn't stay in close enough, all six sensors wouldn't feed the computer the right data and there was no telling what might happen.

Brian sat back in his chair, trying to keep his nerves under control as they waited the last ten minutes. He knew everyone was busy checking and double-checking the plan. He had talked with Dot privately thirty minutes before, telling her to be careful and that he loved her.

She just laughed that wonderful, young laugh of hers, and said, "Trust me, I'm not missing the dancing tonight for anything."

Dot loved to dance, more than anything in life it seemed at times.

And he loved to dance with her.

"Moon crossing the border now, Captain," Marian said.

Brian nodded to Carl who opened a fleet-wide communications link.

"Move into positions now."

On the screen in front of him Brian could see the six other *EPL* warships with their sleek noses and wing-like appearance move as one, turning toward the large moon and matching speed with it.

EPL warships had been designed to look like birds not only to allow them atmospheric flight if needed, but because in so many of the cultures the *EPL* fought against, birds were feared.

Including with the Dogs.

Brian kept *The Bad Business* outside and above the group, moving with them to match the speed of the moon.

They all looked very small against the huge size of the moon, like real birds hovering over a large open area.

Then, almost as a practiced dance in space, the six ships broke away from each other and moved in over an area of the large moon.

The closer it got, Brian could see that it did look a great deal like their moon at home. It had no atmosphere and was covered with impact craters. And it was just about the same size.

Brian took *The Bad Business* in right over the center of the moon and matched the moon's speed and acceleration to stay in position.

"Thirty seconds," Marian said.

"Signal when in position," Brian ordered the other ships.

Each ship had to hover no more than a football field length above the surface where the sensor was, and match the increasing speed of the moon at the same time.

Very, very tricky flying and a slight miss and the *EPL* warship would crash into the moon's surface, or be too far away to intercept the signal.

Brian could see *The Blooming Rose* turn and settle into its assigned position above the moon surface. Dot would be flying it. She had one of the steadiest hands at the helm of a ship that he had ever seen.

Three other warships signaled ready.

Then Dot signaled *The Blooming Rose* was in position and steady.

"Ready here," Brian said, checking to make sure his people were ready with the computer download and new signal into the moon's computer.

At the same moment the other two ships reported they were in position and stable.

"Hold and be ready to turn with the moon," Brian said.

"Intercept signal," Brian ordered the other ships.

As one all turned green that they had the sensor signal.

Then he turned to Marian. "Feed it."

Her fingers flew over the panel and the new programming for the Dog's computer was fed through all six sensors.

An instant later the moon started to turn off its course for Earth.

"Stay with it, everyone," Brian commanded to the other ships as he moved *The Bad Business* to maintain position and keep the feed to the other ships constant.

The moon kept turning and somehow the *EPL* warships held their positions.

"We got some swearing and close calls," Carl said, "but everyone's holding."

"Ten more seconds," Marian said. "And the virus will be loaded."

At five seconds Brian counted it down for the other Captains.

"Five. Four. Three. Two. One."

Marian signaled cut.

"Get out of there now!" Brian shouted to the other pilots.

As one, the other pilots moved their ships up and away from the rough surface of the moon.

Brian had *The Bad Business* moving with them, pushing the ship as fast as he could to try to reach a safe distance.

Twenty seconds later the moon vanished into Trans-Galactic drive space, headed back into the Dog's territory and right for a large military base.

"Clear," Carl said. "All ships made it out of the wash zone from the drive."

Brian slumped in his chair, just smiling as both Carl and Marian applauded and laughed.

Somehow, Earth had dodged that moon.

Barely.

Chapter Nineteen

September 3rd, 2021
Equivalent Earth Time
Location: Deep Space

BRIAN LOOKED DOWN into the wonderful brown eyes of Dot and smiled. "One more dance?"

Around them the music of the last slow song had just died off and a few remaining crew members from other ships were slowly working their way toward the doors that led to the transport ship. The huge ballroom that had been an ongoing party for days was now mostly empty.

She laughed, the sound high and wonderful and something he needed to remember in the long days and nights at the nursing home.

"Our bus is going to leave without us," she said after kissing him quickly.

"Let it," he said, pulling her close and enjoying the feel of her against him.

Since they had turned the moon weapon back on the Dogs, the general had allowed all seven *EPL* warships to dock at Stevens Base for some well-deserved time off while in younger bodies.

Brian and Dot had spent the first night dancing until they had no energy left to even drag themselves out onto the floor.

They had gone back to his room on the base and found a lot more energy. The next day they had spent in meetings with the general and others, then dancing more that evening, then back to her room for the night.

He kissed her again, then together they turned and walked hand-in-hand to the big double doors of the large room, not saying anything.

In fact, they said nothing all the way down the corridor that seemed to stretch for a good mile, then up into their transport. He just wanted to enjoy her company and walking with her.

He needed to remember it all.

He kissed Dot one more time at her cabin door.

"Help me with my applesauce in the morning?" he asked

She smiled. "Always."

Then like two kids saying goodnight after a date in high school, she stepped inside and closed the door.

He walked slowly to his cabin and took off his uniform.

He loved putting it on every mission. He hated taking it off because that meant he wouldn't be young.

He wanted to stay young, to keep serving Earth and defending the *League*.

Going back to his old body was part of that, but not a part he liked.

He slipped back into his old nightshirt and crawled into the coffin-like chamber and pulled the lid closed.

The next thing he remembered, he was being lifted by Lieutenant Kennison from his sleep chamber.

His old stroke-damaged body now part of him again.

Dot and Lieutenant Sherri met them at the transport chamber.

Brian so wanted to reach out to touch Dot's hand, but he could no longer move his arms hardly at all.

The warm thick, humid air of the Chicago night hit him as the transport beam let them go in the nursing home center court.

Above him the golden moon was full in the late summer night air.

He stared up at it as the lieutenant carried him toward his room.

"Not so pretty any more, is it?" Dot said softly from behind him.

She was right.

It wasn't.

After this mission, he wasn't sure if he would ever look up at the moon in the same way again.

It was amazing how seeing the universe and defending Earth could change a person's perspective on things in such a short time.

Simple things like staring up at the moon.

The Last Mission
Seven Months Later

Chapter Twenty

April 19th, 2022
Actual Earth Time
Location: Chicago

DOT PUSHED HER wheelchair ahead of her into the breakfast room of Shady Valley Nursing Home. The big room where she and Brian ate three of their meals every day smelled like pancakes and eggs this fine clear spring day. One morning she had come in and actually smelled bacon, but that had only been a special treat for one resident on his birthday.

She had never liked bacon that much, but the smell had been heavenly.

She liked the warm feeling of the room full of twenty tables set up like a restaurant. Outside the open windows and brown drapes that were tied back and open, she could see the spring starting to bloom on Chicago, and the sun was shining, putting everyone in a light mood.

It felt like the long winter was over.

She could feel it as well.

She got most of the way to her normal table, pushing her wheelchair ahead of her through the obstacle course of the tables and chairs, when she looked up and realized Brian wasn't in his place yet.

Her stomach twisted slightly at the empty place where the nurse would wheel Brian up in his wheelchair and tuck a bib on him. Then three meals a day Dot would help feed him.

It always amazed her how much she loved that man, both in his old form and when he was young, the handsome Captain Brian Saber, and they were in deep space fighting for the survival of Earth.

What mattered to her was that incredible brain and his strength and caring. Old body or young body, she loved Brian.

She had never thought she would find love again in her life. But she had and now just having him late for breakfast bothered her more than she wanted to admit.

When Janice, the orderly, brought her normal two eggs, two pancakes, and orange juice, Dot asked her, "Where's Brian?"

He's a little under the weather this morning," Janice said, "so he's still in bed.

Alarm bells went off in Dot's mind and her stomach twisted into a knot. If Brian died here, from another stroke, or a heart attack, she would lose him forever.

That stroke that had taken the last of his movement a year or so ago had scared her more than she wanted to think about right now. He had survived it, but barely. Another one like that he wouldn't survive.

It was one thing to watch his ship go into battle because she knew that if he died in battle, defending Earth, he wouldn't mind.

But he couldn't die of old age in a nursing home. Not the great Captain Brian Saber, the most decorated Captain ever in the history of the *Earth Protection League*.

She left most of her breakfast and headed back down the hall toward their rooms. Her room was across the hall from his and it hadn't occurred to her to see if he was there when she left.

She hurried as fast as her damaged legs would allow her, pushing her wheelchair ahead of her. The trip down the hallway seemed to stretch, but eventually she got to his door and eased it open.

His room was dark and she could hear his labored breathing.

"Oh, thank God," she said softly to herself.

He was covered by a sheet, and his frail, old body seemed tiny on the large hospital bed.

She moved into the room silently, letting the door close gently behind her, dropping the room into a dimness lit only by the nightlight from the open bathroom door.

She moved over beside him and brushed his rough cheek gently.

He didn't wake up.

She sat in her wheelchair, facing his bed.

This was where she belonged.

At his side.

Chapter Twenty-one

April 20th, 2022
Actual Earth Time
Location: Chicago

"CAPTAIN LEEDS," the young, female voice said in a very gentle tone.

There was a mission tonight. Oh, thank heavens. She would get to see Brian again and talk with him about what they were going to do to get him out of the nursing home before another stroke took him from her.

She had sat all day, off and on, beside his bed as he slept, only leaving to use the bathroom and go to lunch and then dinner.

But at both she hadn't felt like eating much at all. It wasn't the same sitting there without Brian.

Finally, Joyce, the night nurse, had woken her early in the evening since she had fallen asleep in her wheelchair beside Brian, her head on his bed beside him. The nurse had convinced her to go to bed even though she didn't want to leave Brian's side.

Lieutenant Sherri picked up Dot in her strong arms and moved quickly, but carefully, across the hall and into Brian's room, then toward the sliding glass door that led into the center courtyard.

Brian was still in the bed, sleeping.

"Isn't Captain Saber coming on this mission?"

"He is not," Sherri said. "I honestly don't know why."

Dot felt her stomach twist into a knot and she almost told Sherri to put her back to bed. She had never gone on a mission without Brian and she didn't want this to be the first.

"Stop for a moment, Lieutenant," Dot said, her voice firm and almost an order. Sherri did as instructed.

Dot needed a moment to think this through.

She glanced at Brian's old wall clock that ticked like a bomb, filling his room with a constant reminder of time passing. *Three-sixteen in the morning.*

She would be back shortly in Earth time. Maybe fifteen or twenty minutes at the most, even though she might spend days or weeks on the mission. Somehow the weirdness of the space travel could bring her back just a short time after she left.

So she wouldn't be gone that long in nursing home time.

Brian seemed to be resting peacefully, his breathing normal. Maybe it was right to not stress him with a mission and tire him out even more if he wasn't feeling well.

Plus, if she left for these few minutes, it would allow her to talk with someone in the *League*, get them to get Brian out of here before he died. Surely there was something the most decorated captain in the *Earth Protection League* could do in deep space in a young, healthy body.

So going on the mission would be her best chance to help Brian. She would talk

with someone as soon as the mission was over.

If she lived, that was.

If some alien didn't kill her first.

"I'm ready," Lieutenant," she said with one long look at Brian.

She had once figured up that in the last four years of going on missions, she had actually got to live another fourteen years of life in space, young again. And every extra minute had been wonderful. Scary at times, but wonderful.

And all of it had been with Brian.

The first year, until she earned her own ship, she had served on Brian's ship.

They had danced so many times.

She didn't want that to end now.

She wouldn't let it if she had anything to say about it.

The sliding door to the outside slid silently open and the Chicago early spring air bit hard against her old skin. Lieutenant Sherri didn't even pause at the door other than to slide it quickly and silently closed.

They were only in the cold air for a moment before a yellow beam of light lifted them both quickly into the transport ship that was cloaked above the nursing home.

Dot knew that around the country the same thing had happened, or was happening, at least forty-one other times as the crew of *The Blooming Rose* was gathered from their perspective nursing homes and retirement apartments. A couple of them even lived in the same nursing home, which General Brooks had once said made things a lot easier, but was too dangerous for the most part to have more than two because if their entire ship was lost, the league didn't want to try to explain why half of the population of a nursing home died suddenly one night.

She couldn't imagine going on missions without Brian there as well to talk with. Although for years before she had known about the league, he had gone on missions and not told her a word.

Lieutenant Sherri quickly carried Dot down the hallway in the ship to a room with a silver, coffin-shaped sleep chamber and laid Dot down slowly on the soft cushions inside.

Dot loved the symbol of the coffin allowing her to be young again. It made her smile every time.

The young lieutenant patted her shoulder. "Have a good trip, Captain."

Then she closed the lid on the coffin and tapped it twice as a signal to Dot that it was secure. In this old body, it didn't matter. Dot wouldn't have been able to even push the lid open if she tried.

A moment later the orange and rose-smelling gas filled the chamber and she drifted off into the sleep of the dead.

Her coffin would be transferred to her ship *The Blooming Rose* with the rest of her crew in deep space.

Only then would she discover what was so important as to pull her away from the man she loved.

Chapter Twenty-two

April 20th, 2022
Equivalent Earth Time
Location: Deep Space

THE TOP OF the coffin snapped open with a hiss and cool oxygen bathed over her face. Captain Dot Leeds snapped her eyes open, then held her arms up to look at them. What she saw was the young skin and shapes of youth.

She flexed her fingers and the muscles under the skin rippled.

It felt wonderful.

It always felt wonderful.

No pain, no aches.

Just the sense of health and youth.

She had made it again.

The room smelled faintly of oranges and roses mingled with machine oil, and she loved both smells. She had called her ship *The Blooming Rose* because of that smell.

With both hands, she grabbed the sides of the coffin sleep module and lifted herself out, kicking over the side without so much as a caught heel. The feeling of youth was simply wonderful, better than any drug ever invented.

She still wore her old woman's nightgown, but she quickly pulled that off and tossed it back in the coffin. She would need it for the return trip, if she lived through this coming fight. If not, they'd need it for her body. And tomorrow morning her son on the west coast would get a call that she had died peacefully in her sleep.

But she had no plans on dying this mission. She wouldn't do that to Brian. She wouldn't leave him there alone to die in his old body. That wasn't going to happen.

She flexed the muscles in her shoulders and neck. Her body was one she barely remembered from her youth. Yet each time she went on a mission, this body returned, good as ever. Whatever the strange relative-matter-physics involved in Trans-Galactic travel, she loved this body, and hadn't appreciated it enough back when she was young.

At least she hadn't appreciated it in the right ways.

She got dressed and then brushed a hand through her now full head of brown hair. Then she turned and glanced at the only mirror in the small room.

The reflection that greeted her was one of her youth, control, and power. She couldn't be more than twenty-one or twenty-two on this mission. Only the knowledge and memories inside the young body were of an eighty-seven year old woman who had, seemingly moments before, been asleep in a nursing home room in Chicago, on the planet Earth.

No telling exactly where in space she was at the moment.

She looked twenty-one, but was a four-year veteran of the *Earth Protection League*. Earth time.

She had earned her ship and her captain's rank faster than even Brian had done. Brian's advice and guidance had been amazing and part of that quick rise to being a Captain.

One nice thing about being in the *EPL*. Out here it didn't matter how young you looked. Just that you got the job done.

She patted the stunner on her hip, enjoying the solid feel of the hard-rubber handle. Years ago she never would have thought she could ever fire a gun, let alone enjoy feeling one on her hip.

With one more quick look in the mirror, she turned and strode out of the room, turning right toward the Command Center of *The Blooming Rose.*

She had a mission to finish and people to talk to before getting back to Brian and getting him out of that nursing home.

She knew this ship like the back of her now-young hand. She had been on board it for almost a hundred missions, had renamed it when she became captain, had flown it through some of the toughest space in this sector of the Galaxy. It felt like home, far more than her home back in Chicago had ever done. In fact, her cabin on this ship was twice the size as her nursing home room.

The hallways of the ship were wide enough that three people could walk side-by-side. The metal walls were covered in a rubber coating and painted light blue which made them feel warm and soft and inviting, not like walking down the corridor of a normal military ship.

She also loved the floors. They were all coated in a thicker rubber substance that kept noise down and were still solid under a person's feet. Only problem was that one person could sneak up on another easily.

Every twenty paces was a communications screen on the wall for instant contract from anywhere in the ship and every forty paces was a sliding bulkhead door hidden in the walls that could be closed to shut off sections of the ship.

Throughout the ship her crew would be coming awake in their cabins, dressing and moving to their stations, getting ready for whatever faced them on this mission.

She didn't wait for them, but instead strode directly to the empty Command Center and dropped down into the captain's chair.

Her chair.

Around her the fairly small room was only three other stations, one on her left, the other on her right, both with a high-backed chair like hers and view screens above them showing the blackness of space and seven other *EPL* warships.

The fourth station was behind her, the communication station. She never had anyone in that spot, letting her two command crew do that job.

Brian did the same on his ship.

Coming in June

from all your favorite booksellers
in trade paper and electronic editions.

Actually, the Command Center was on the very front and highest point of the warship. And the ship itself was so big that even at a good pace it was a good five-minute hike from the Command Center to the engine room at the back of the warship.

And the ship itself, as all *EPL* battleships, was shaped like a bird. It seemed that many of Earth's enemies found birds frightening creatures.

In front of her a small screen on the panel flared to light and the smiling face of General George Meyers filled it. He had deep blue eyes, white hair, and more wrinkles than almost any human Dot had ever seen. Yet the face was one that seemed comfortable with command. She had no idea where he was located, in what part of space. For all she knew, he could be back on Earth, but she didn't think so.

"Glad you made it, Captain Leeds."

"Glad to be here, sir," Dot said. "I'm going to need to talk with you about Captain Saber after this is finished."

The General nodded. "Of course."

"So what is the problem?"

She expected the normal mission briefing, but was shocked when the General said, "Not yet. I need you to gather with seven other Captains on Captain Saber's ship. His second in command, Marian Knudson has the helm for this mission."

"When?" Dot asked.

She had spent a lot of time on Brian's ship, but never once when he wasn't on it.

"Twenty minutes," he said and the screen went blank.

"What was that all about?" Steve "Quick Draw" Oldham asked as he dropped into his chair in the station to her right.

Steve was her second-in-command and had been her close friend for years now, even turning down his own ship to stay with her as a team. He lived in a nursing home in California somewhere. On Earth he was three years younger than she was. He looked like a teenager on this mission. It seems they had really pushed them out farther away from Earth than normal.

Steve had gotten his nickname in basic camp because he could draw a photon stunner faster than even the instructor and was a deadly shot with it. Watching too many Roy Rogers westerns when he was a kid, he had said. The nickname had stuck.

"Not a clue," Dot said, shaking her head.

She didn't like having to get with other captains and without Brian to lead them. It meant something real ugly was happening.

She stood as her third-in-command came in.

Carrie Nelson lived in the Chicago area as well, but out near the airport, and was about Dot's age on Earth. Out in space she was a petite little blonde who couldn't be more than five-two at best. Dot at five-six seemed to tower over her.

Yet Dot had seen Carrie in a fight. She was like a whirlwind and if Dot had to pick Steve or Carrie to have her back when things got ugly in hand-to-hand, she would pick Carrie.

"A little meeting first," Dot said to Carrie's puzzled look. "Got to go over to Captain Saber's ship."

She smiled. "Not too much time I hope."

Captain Saber is not along on this mission," Dot said. "Not feeling well."

"Oh," was all Carrie said, looking at Dot with a compassionate look.

"Don't worry," Dot said, smiling at her friend and third-in-command. "I'll get his ass out of that nursing home when we get done here."

"So who's driving *The Bad Business?*" Steve asked.

"Marian Knudson is acting Captain," Dot said.

"I hear she's a red-headed dream on two legs," Carrie said, laughing and winking at Dot. "You should take Steve along. He needs to get laid once before he dies."

Steve put his hand up in the air. "I volunteer for that duty."

Dot shook her head. "I have a hunch Acting Captain Knudson makes it a habit to not sleep with anyone with Quick in their reputation."

She winked at Carrie who could barely contain her laughter with her back to Steve's frown.

"Get the ship up and ready to go," Dot said, smiling at her two friends. "I'll be back shortly. I have a hunch we're in some deep trouble with this mission."

And whatever they were facing, she was going to beat it and get back to Earth and Brian, one way or another.

Chapter Twenty-three

April 20th, 2022
Equivalent Earth Time
Location: Deep Space

DOT STOPPED BESIDE the other six captains, all of whom she already knew well, as Acting-Captain Knudson walked to the front of the room that the crew used for mostly dances and watching movies.

Dot and Brian had spent a lot of time in this room after missions, dancing and talking.

Right now the big movie screen had been extended from the wall and everyone was facing the screen.

The silence in the room felt like that of a funeral. Dot just hoped it wasn't going to be all of their funerals they were attending.

Marian clicked the intercom. "Go ahead, Carl."

A moment later General Bank's face filled the big screen. The General didn't wear his normal smile as he said, "Good morning, captains. We have an ugly situation at hand."

Dot stood back to one side and tried to focus on what the General was saying and not worry about Brian.

Almost impossible to do.

"The Dogs have broken through once again," the general said. "It seems our destroying their base sort of made them angry."

"What?" Dot asked, stunned. The other captains all shifted and shook their heads in understanding.

The general went on. "They broke through our outer defenses yesterday Earth time. We've had a few skirmishes with them along the border over the last few days, but this breakthrough now is major. Our allies in the *League* and border patrols couldn't stop them and had to pull back."

"That bad, huh?" Dot asked. A feeling of dread was quickly replacing the wonderful feel of being young again.

The general nodded. "This morning we got data that make it clear that they are headed to Earth to destroy the center of the *League* once and for all. And they have enough ships to do it."

Dot stepped forward toward the big screen and looked intently at the general, not letting the worry filling her chest show. Since without Brian here, she was the most senior captain in the group. She felt it was her job to ask the questions.

"How many ships did they send?"

"Over five hundred of their warships got through the border and are headed for your position at a very slow, but still Trans-Galactic speed," the general said. "Your job is to try to slow them down even more, give us time behind you to form a second and third line of defense to turn them and keep them from reaching Earth."

"Understood," Dot said.

"Anyone have any questions?" the general asked

Dot glanced at the other captains.

All looked firm and determined. But none of the captains seemed to want to say anything.

She turned back to the general. "We'll slow them down. Maybe knock their numbers down a few. You can count on that."

The general nodded. "I knew I could depend on all of you."

The screen went blank.

She took a deep breath, stunned. At least the general had the common decency to not say that it had been nice knowing them all. Or even good luck.

This would be the last mission for all of them.

The general knew it. They all knew it. This was their funeral.

She would not make it back to see Brian again.

That thought just broke her heart and she shuddered.

She would die young and in deep space, just as Brian had always hoped he would. Better than in his sleep in the nursing home back on Earth. So that meant that if he wasn't going to die there, she had to win this coming battle somehow.

She took a deep breath, shoved the fear aside, and turned to the other captains. "Looks like we've got some work ahead of us."

She strolled for the door, headed for her Command Center.

If this was her last mission and she would never see Brian again, she intended to make it a good one.

If she had anything to say about it, she was going to save Earth one last time.

And the man she loved in the process.

Chapter Twenty-four

April 20th, 2022
Equivalent Earth Time
Location: Deep Space

"SO, HOW WAS the dreamboat Acting Captain Knudson?" Carrie asked as Dot entered *The Blooming Rose* command center. "Steve here can't seem to concentrate."

"You know I'm here, don't you?" Steve said.

"Ignoring you like usual," Carrie said, staring at Dot. "You look upset, Captain. Was it that bad?"

"This mission sucks."

She dropped down into her command chair and just stared at the screen showing the empty space around them and the other seven *EPL* warships.

"So what do they have us doing this time?" Steve asked. "Can't be much worse than those reptile things we had to clean up on Darren Six last mission."

"The Dogs got pissed at us for sending a moon at their military base and broke out of their fence," Dot said. "We're supposed to try to slow them down until the *League* can mount a decent defense behind us."

"Crap," Steve said.

"You're kidding, right?" Carrie asked.

Dot didn't turn to look at her second-in-command. She knew that Carrie's face would be white.

"How many?" Steve asked, his voice low and hushed.

"Five hundred of their warships. Eight of us."

"Oh, for a moment there I thought we were in trouble," Steve said.

"Does the League have any idea how we're supposed to do this?" Carrie asked.

"Not a word," Dot said, smiling at her friend. "They left it up to our ancient wisdom to come up with something to slow them down."

"I hate it when they do that," Steve said.

"Yeah, me too," Dot said, trying not to laugh. Thank God for friends around her. They always made things easier in the toughest situations.

"You two work on finding out how much time we have until they get here, what speed they're moving, so on, and I'll brief the rest of the crew. Call them all to the rec room, would you, Steve?"

She pushed herself easily to her feet and headed out.

She could have done this task from her command chair, but she wanted to feel young again, walk quickly again, just one more time.

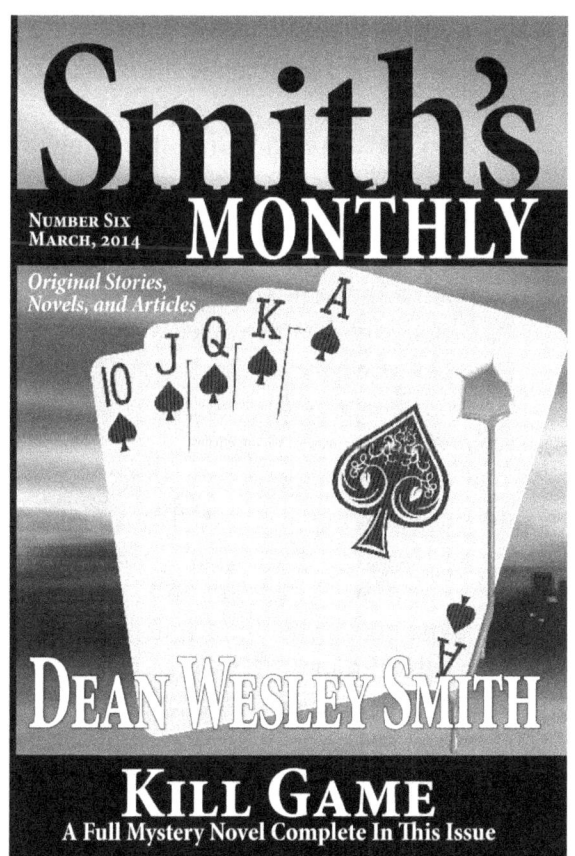

And besides, her crew deserved to learn they were about to die from her personally.

It was the least she could do.

It was halfway through the personnel briefing with the almost forty members of his gathered crew that Dot came up with the plan that just might give them a little better chance of staying alive a little longer.

And maybe in the long run, save Earth.

A few minutes later she finished the briefing and sprinted back to the Command Center of the ship, her shoes making almost no sound on the rubber floors of the hallways

She enjoyed the run, but then finally dropped into her chair. Wow, she loved being young, being in shape, being able to just walk. Let alone run.

"How long?"

"Five hundred Dog Warships will be barking on our front steps in exactly thirty-five minutes," Carrie said.

"Perfect," Dot said.

"Perfect?" Steve asked. "You know have a very weird way of looking at this situation."

Dot laughed. "Steve, contact all the other ships and have them be ready to match the Dog's Trans-Galactic speed in fifteen minutes."

Steve glanced over at her. "You really like getting your butt kicked by slug-looking poodles, don't you?"

"How old are you, Steve?" Dot asked, her fingers working on the board as she talked.

"Six months short of the big eighty-five," Steve said. "And still getting around just fine with the ladies at the home I might add."

"They can't be very picky," Carrie said.

"And how long did it take us to get from Earth to this position?" Dot asked.

"From what measuring point?" Steve asked.

Dot liked Steve because he understood all the crazy things that went on with space and time on these ships.

"Earth time?" Dot asked.

"Over sixty or so years," Steve said.

"Transport shipboard time? How long did the trip take to get us out here?"

"Six days, ten hours, and a few odd minutes while we slept like babies."

"And it will take us that long to get back?" Dot asked, "Right?"

"Shipboard time," Steve said. "They'll speed up the ship slightly on the return voyage and we'll end up back in our beds less than thirty minutes after we left, Earth time that is, even if we spend weeks out here. You know that."

Dot nodded. It was why she knew she could safely leave Brian sleeping. She was only going to be gone for a few minutes in Brian's time if she survived.

"So how are the Dogs handling the same matter/relativity/time problem on their flight toward Earth at the speeds they are traveling?"

"How the hell would I—"

Suddenly Steve stopped and smiled at Dot. "I see where you're headed Captain. Their life spans are shorter than ours, right?"

"Exactly," Dot said. "Which is why they are moving at a slow Trans-Galactic speed, because they don't dare go any faster or they would end up Dog-pups or not exist at all when they reached Earth."

"Which means they have to be damn old Dogs right now," Steve said, "at the beginning of their flight. They cleared out their Dog nursing homes and have them flying the ships."

"Exactly," Dot said. "And you and I both know how well old Dogs like us move back on Earth."

Steve laughed. "We're young and right now they're old. Really, really old. You're right! Perfect!"

"You know, I think you two are right," Carrie said, shaking her head.

"Scary, huh?" Steve said, smiling.

"Every so often we get one," Dot said, grinning at her second-in-command.

Then Dot turned back to her controls. "I'd say it's time to kick some wrinkled Dog butt, don't you?"

She punched the communications link to the seven captains of the other *League* ships. Quickly, she explained what she had figured out and how they were going to fight the Dogs.

"Launch all single men fighters on my command when we reach attack positions," she said to the captains. Each warship carried a fleet of thirty single fighters.

"Have your pilots keep the single-man fighters on full thrust and constantly turning, diving, retreating," Dot said to the other Captains. "Break the fighters into units of ten with each ten ship unit attacking one dog ship, then moving on. Have them keep moving as fast as they can all the time. The aliens flying those ships are slow and old right now, just as we all were when they brought us out here. Remember that and maybe we can buy the *League* some real time."

All the captains agreed and with a wish of good luck, they all signed off.

Twenty minutes later they launched the single-man fighters.

And a few minutes later the Dog warships appeared on the view screens.

They were ugly, sausage-looking ships, with slick-looking hulls and pro-truding weapons systems and thrusters. The fighters had been ordered to stay away from in front of the weapons and target the thrusters. Their mission was to slow them down and, as Steve had said, there was no better way to do that than shoot a Dog warship in the ass.

Chapter Twenty-five

April 20th, 2022
Equivalent Earth Time
Location: Deep Space

THERE WAS SOMETHING about the formation of Dog warships that bothered Dot, but for the few minutes it took to get her fighters staged around the alien fleet, she couldn't figure it out.

Around her Carrie and Steve were busy keeping *The Blooming Rose* out of reach of the Dogs long-range weapons for a moment. After the fighters had their fun, then it would be time for the big warships to take a run at them.

So she had a moment to just sit and watch the fight, not something she normally liked doing. She had always been much more of a person who waded in and took the lead. But for the moment, the small fighters needed the room to flit around like fleas.

She stared at the formation of the Dog fleet. With their weird long shapes, there was just something about them she couldn't get a handle on.

Then suddenly it struck her.

They were staggered like bowling pins on an alley, with lead ships protecting other ships in the middle of the formation.

The Dog fleet was flying in bowling pin formations, a couple dozen of them per formation.

She and her husband had spent a lot of years bowling with friends a couple times a week until all their families started to get too old and his job kept him too busy. She had loved to bowl.

Not as much as she loved to dance, but since the accident that killed him and crippled her, she hadn't thought of bowling at all, where every night she had dreamed of dancing until Brian got her out here in space and allowed her to be young and dance for real again.

She had loved the smell of the old bowling alley in Chicago she and her husband used to go to, the feel of the silly leather shoes they had to wear, the weight of the ball in her hands. She usually came close to beating her husband most nights, and would have if he wasn't as competitive as she was and a darned fine athlete.

She loved most of all the feeling of getting a strike, sending that big ball right down the center of the pins.

She stared at the Dog ships and understood how they might just make a difference in this fight. It might get them all killed a little faster, but if her idea worked, it would cause huge damage to the Dog fleet.

"You know how to override the Trans-Galactic drive limitations on this ship?" Dot asked, turning to Carrie as the fighters broke into attack groups and swarmed around the oncoming Dog warships like so many bugs on a hot summer's afternoon.

"I think I could do it," Carrie said, frowning and looking at Dot. "Why?"

"I'm just wondering," Dot said. "Tell me what would happen if we plowed right through the middle of that fleet at full Trans-Galactic speed?"

"Besides destroy us?" Carrie said.

"I'm not so sure it would hurt us that bad," Dot said. "If I remember right, at full and complete Trans-Galactic speed, we're on complete force-field shields, big enough to knock just about anything short of a small moon out of the way. I think I'm remembering right from all those confusing lectures back in basic training."

"Actually, our shields would just knock a small hole through a moon," Steve said. "Like drilling from one side to the other."

Carrie stared at Dot for a moment, then glanced back at the big view screen showing the alien fleet.

"They sort of do look like bowling pins, don't they?" Dot asked.

"Bowling for Dogs," Steve said, clapping. "I love it! I haven't been bowling for years."

Carrie set to work to see if she could get complete control of the top speed of the Trans-Galactic drive controls. If anyone in the fleet could do it, Carrie could. In the Command Center they had control over slower Trans-Galactic speeds for short trips and battles like this one, but never full speed. It was just too dangerous to leave in the hands of a bunch of senior citizens, no matter how well-trained.

In thirty seconds, Carrie looked up, smiling. "Got it. Easier than I thought."

On the screen the fighters were having some luck. The Dog warships were firing, but not really hitting anything. The fighters were picking at the thrusters of the ships like a kid picked at a scab.

Two dog ships were already dead in space, left behind by the fleet. But there were already four single-man fighters destroyed, four elderly humans who wouldn't be returning alive to their nursing home rooms tonight on Earth.

In fact, the way those fighters had exploded, replacement bodies would have to be put in those beds to fool the families.

Dot quickly called the other captains and explained her idea, looking for any of them to knock a hole in the idea.

None did.

For a moment they all looked sort of shocked at the idea.

After that, they all just broke into smiles and a couple made really bad bowling jokes.

"Have the fighters pull back and give us plenty of room. We'll give it a shot. Keep them back for five minutes or until you hear from me again," Dot said. "We hope to be coming back the same way."

All acting captains wished her luck and signed off.

"Yup, Acting Captain Knudson is good enough to eat," Carrie said, smiling at Steve. "Five course meal and three desserts."

"Yeah, I do a mean barbeque," Steve said.

"Sloppy and covered in sauce," Carrie said. "Figures."

"When you are ready," Dot said to her first officer as she shook her head.

"Not too far," Steve said.

"I'll be careful," Carrie said, smiling at Steve. "Last thing I want is to have to change your diapers."

Dot, on instructions from Carrie, carefully sat the Trans-Galactic drive for only a six second burst. That would take them through the Dog Warship fleet and some distance beyond, but not too far. Too far and they might end up too young to pilot the ship back into position. Or worse, end up in Dog territory beyond the border.

Then Dot moved *The Blooming Rose* around and to a position a distance in front of the Dog fleet.

"Ready to lose a little age and wrinkles?" Dot asked.

"And with luck, a few Dog Warships in the process," Steve said.

"Right down the lane," Carrie said. "Go for the strike."

Dot punched the T-G Drive engage, and for the first time in all the missions, she saw what space looked like at full Trans-Galactic speed.

It was a blur of black and white streaks.

Nothing more.

Not even pretty.

Just weird.

She was glad she normally slept through it.

Then as quickly as it started, it ended and the stars were back, solid in space.

There was no sign of the Dog Warships, or the rest of the *League* fleet.

"Damage report?" Dot asked.

"Nothing major," Steve said as his fingers flew over his board, checking everything.

"Some really minor strain on the shields, but they are holding fine at ninety-eight percent," Carrie said.

"Where are we?" Dot asked.

"We've gone a bunch closer to the Dog Border and we're four weeks younger than a few seconds ago," Carrie said.

"I knew I felt better," Dot said. "Don't you just love how this relativity and mass and time stuff works?"

"Yeah," Steve said. "Just wish I really understood it."

"I hear you there," Dot said.

"Thank heavens one of us on this ship does," Carrie said, laughing.

Dot didn't argue with that at all.

Dot flipped the ship over and, with a quick run of her fingers over the board, reset the controls to return them to just a few seconds after they had left and just a slight distance farther ahead of the Dog fleet to make up for the speed of the Dog ships.

"Getting older," Dot said.

Again the view screens showed black and white streaks for a long six seconds, then normal space returned.

"Damage?" Dot asked.

"No more than last time," Carrie said. "Shields at ninety-seven percent."

"Holy cow!" Steve said. "I think we got a strike."

"Maybe two," Dot said, staring at the damage they had done to the Dogs. They had punched not just one, but two holes in the fleet of Dog warships, damaging and destroying at least thirty of them in the process.

And the single-man fighters were now swooping in to take advantage of the confusion to cause even more damage.

For the first time since Dot heard about the mission, she felt there might be a chance she would see Brian again.

Just a chance.

But there was a lot of work to do.

"Get ready to hit them again," Dot said. "Tell the fighters to get out of the way in thirty seconds. We're coming through."

As they waited the few seconds for the fighters to again withdraw, Steve said, "They're going to come up with a terrible name for this, you know."

"And what would that be?" Dot asked

"The Leeds' Yo-Yo Maneuver," Steve said.

"Sounds good to me," Dot said, laughing.

"Nah," Carrie said. "I think it will be the Leeds' Bowling Maneuver."

Dot waited until the other pilots confirmed that they were ready and the fight-ers were out of the way, then she punched them back into full Trans-Galactic speed once again, aiming directly at the thickest part of the Dog fleet.

And for a few seconds, she got even younger.

And she really, really loved being young.

She just needed the man she loved here beside her to make this perfect.

Chapter Twenty-Six

April 20th, 2022
Equivalent Earth Time
Location: Deep Space

AFTER EVERYTHING WAS cleaned up, and she had sent Carrie and Steve to get some dinner and enjoy the coming party, Dot put in a call to General Banks.

"Captain Leeds," the general said, nodding as he came on the screen. His face was again smiling, the wrinkles that surrounded his eyes and mouth clear once again. "Great job out there."

"Thank you, General," she said. "But I'm worried about Captain Saber."

He nodded and his expression became serious. "We are watching his condition very closely. If you hadn't been able to stop the Dogs, we would have taken a chance and pulled him to lead a second line of defense."

Dot nodded. That made sense to her. If they could let him rest, they would, but if they couldn't, why not have the best Captain in the fleet fighting a second line of defense for Earth, even if it endangered his life.

"So if his condition worsens, what are you going to do?"

"Captain," the General said, his voice firm, his eyes intent. "We have our procedures and our rules and all of us are bound by them, including Captain Saber."

She started to say something, but he held up his hand. "I have been told Captain Saber is stronger. We are watching his condition. Again, great job today."

With that he clicked off, leaving the screen blank in front of her.

Somehow she managed to not put her fist through the blank screen.

Then she almost called him back, but decided that until she got back and understood what was really going on with Brian, she didn't dare. She might have just saved all of Earth, but it didn't seem that the *EPL* was going to be very grateful with the man she loved.

The man who had saved them all many more times than she had.

She didn't dance that night at the party, but instead just sat and drank and watched Acting Captain Marian Knudson and Dot's third-in-command, Steve, flirt. They were clearly good together.

And Steve made Marian laugh, which from what Brian had told Dot, was unusual.

Dot wondered how many people had watched her and Brian do the same thing over the last few years.

Finally, it was time to head back.

Normally she hated going in and putting on her old nightgown and going back to her old body. But this time she was anxious to be old again.

Brian was there.

And spending even another minute without him wasn't something she really wanted to do.

She crawled into her sleep coffin and closed the lid, letting the gas knock her out.

A moment later she was being picked up from the coffin by Lieutenant Sherri.

"Good mission, Captain?" the Lieutenant asked.

"We got the job done," Dot said.

What seemed like only a moment later she was being carried through the chill evening air of Chicago and into Brian's room.

He still seemed to be sleeping comfortably.

The lieutenant carried Dot across the hallway and put her in her wheelchair as Dot instructed.

"Have a good night, Captain," Lieutenant Sherri said, snapping off a salute and heading back across the hall and out the door.

Dot waited a moment, then wheeled her chair across the hallway and into Brian's room.

She reached up and touched his arm and he stirred slightly, but kept sleeping.

She moved in close to his bed, locked the brakes on her chair, and put her head down on his bed next to him.

Somehow, she had to save him.

She could save all of Earth.

Why couldn't she save the man she loved?

Chapter Twenty-seven

April 20th, 2022
Actual Earth Time
Location: Chicago

AN HOUR LATER Joyce, the night nurse, woke her and helped her across the hallway and into her own bed. She didn't think she would be able to sleep because she was so worried, but she did, waking at her normal time.

After her morning bath and dressing, she pushed her wheelchair ahead of her out into the hallway, working to get her old legs loosened up a little. She had to see how Brian was doing, then get a little breakfast and come back to sit with him.

Two people she didn't recognize were talking in whispers in the hallway and Brian's door was closed. One was a middle-aged man, the other a younger woman. Both had on dark winter coats and jeans. The woman had dark brown hair pulled back and stuffed in the collar of her coat.

The man was tall and held himself with great posture, his thinning brown hair combed back and slightly long. The younger woman looked like she might be his daughter.

"Is Brian all right?" Dot asked, her stomach twisting into a hard knot as she moved toward them and Brian's door.

He couldn't have died in the middle of the night. He just couldn't have.

"We're not sure," the middle-aged man said, stepping away from the young girl with a nod.

The girl smiled at Dot and then turned and headed for the nurse's station down the hall.

The man stuck out his hand and smiled. "I'm Brian Wilson Saber, Brian's oldest son. But I have always gone by Wilson. And yes, my dad loved the Beach Boys. You must be Dot Leeds."

"I am," she said, shaking Wilson's hand.

Now that he said it, she could see the clear likeness. She only knew Brian young or old. Not middle-aged, which is why she hadn't seen the resemblance with his son instantly.

But he was clearly as handsome as his father. Brian had talked about Wilson at times and told her that someday he would make a great Captain.

"Nice meeting you," Wilson said, shaking her hand gently and then releasing it. "Dad has talked a lot about you."

"I hope all good," she said, smiling.

"All very good," he said, smiling back with Brian's smile.

"So what do you mean you're not sure how Brian is?" she asked.

"My daughter has headed to the lunchroom to get something to eat," Wilson said. "How about we go there and you can have some breakfast and I'll try to explain what the doctors have said."

She nodded. At least Brian's son was willing to help her and get her into the loop. That was a start. She would have to be very careful to not say anything to him about the *EPL*. Even though Brian had said Wilson would be a good Captain some day, he hadn't told her that he knew about the *EPL*. And he didn't need to know that she hoped to save his father by getting him out of here somehow and into deep space.

To Brian's son, that would not be saving him, since his father would be considered dead at that point.

But Dot had no other choice. She had to save the man she loved by killing him in his son's eyes.

Wilson walked with her slowly down the hall and into the lunchroom. Again the bright room smelled of pancakes and eggs. The drapes were all open showing the bright Chicago spring morning outside the windows. She had always loved Chicago in the spring, especially after a hard winter. It always felt like a rebirth.

After she met Brian's granddaughter, a young woman named Sue who worked

Now Available
from all your favorite booksellers
in trade paper and electronic editions.

as a head nurse at another nursing home about ten miles away, Dot steered the conversation back to Brian.

Neither one of them let on that they knew about the EPL, so she was careful.

Wilson looked worried, an expression she had seen on his father's face many times.

"The doctor thinks Dad may have had another small stroke yesterday," Wilson said. "He wants Dad to rest and his condition is now being monitored every few hours by the nurses here."

Dot took a deep breath and let it out slowly. "That doesn't sound good, does it?"

"We honestly don't know," Wilson said and his daughter nodded. Brian's granddaughter clearly had some medical knowledge as a nurse and that was who Dot would turn to.

"Any idea how long?" Dot asked Sue after they paused for their breakfasts to be delivered. Dot had her normal eggs and pancakes and both Wilson and his daughter had a glass of orange juice and toast.

"He might get a little stronger and last for another two or three years," Sue said. "The kind of small strokes he suffers are that way. We just have to see what is happening with him, and if he gains strength in the next day or so."

So that was what the brass in charge of the *Earth Protection League* were hoping. They wanted their top front-line fighter to get better here and keep going on missions for them.

But if he didn't, that's what worried Dot. She had no idea if the *League* would just let him die at that point.

"I'll watch him as much as I'm able," Dot said.

"Thank you," Wilson said. "I know dad would appreciate that."

Dot nodded and tried to force herself to eat. If she was going to sit with Brian, she needed to keep her strength up.

That last thing either of them needed was for her to get sick as well.

Chapter Twenty-eight

April 23rd, 2022
Actual Earth Time
Location: Chicago

THE LAST TWO days had been a total nightmare for Dot. She had spent her day either resting beside Brian or eating the three meals she didn't want to eat or even taste.

Both Wilson and Sue stopped in at least twice a day and often sat with Brian as well. Dot had talked to them, but no one else.

Sue was getting worried that Brian wasn't getting better. He hadn't really even woken up in the last two days other than to moan and shift slightly. He seemed to be stuck and sometimes his breathing got so raspy, Dot wasn't sure if he was going to make it for another ten minutes.

If Sue, who was a full nurse, was worried, that just terrified Dot.

She hoped that in some way the *League* was watching. But she wasn't sure how they could be. No one talked to her at all.

Dot was starting to become convinced they were just going to let Brian die.

By the morning of the third day, she was emotionally drained, and getting more tired by the hour.

At one point, she fell asleep sitting in her chair with her head on Brian's bed beside him, and she dreamed once again of dancing.

Since she had learned of the *League* and Brian had danced with her, the dreams of dancing, of being free, hadn't come back.

She wasn't sure what that meant.

But now they were back.

Finally, on the morning of the third day, Brian woke up.

She had just returned from breakfast and sitting next to Brian's bed in her wheelchair.

Wilson was reading a magazine in another chair he had pulled in from somewhere.

Other than to nod hello, they hadn't talked.

Brian moaned and opened his eyes.

Then he looked at Dot and smiled.

But it wasn't the vibrant smile of the man she loved, but instead the smile of a man saying goodbye.

She jumped to her feet and leaned forward in case he wanted to try to talk.

He tried to whisper, but clearly his throat was dry.

She quickly got him an ice chip from the cup of ice she kept near his head and gave it to him to wet his lips.

Wilson was standing behind her, watching.

Brian smiled and nodded, then said, "I see you two have finally met."

"She's as wonderful as you said, Dad," Wilson said.

Brian smiled weakly. "I know."

Then Brian tried to say something more, but it came out only a whisper.

She leaned down to hear him better.

"Marry me," he said. "Please. I want to go dancing."

"Of course," she said.

He sighed and said, "Good."

Then he closed his eyes and for a moment Dot thought he was gone.

Finally, his rough breathing resumed, but barely.

Dot stood upright, holding for balance onto the thin arm of the man she loved, listening to him struggle for breath. She couldn't believe what he had just asked.

They had talked about spending their lives together, but never about marriage. Why now?

There was something she was missing.

"What did he say?" Wilson asked.

Dot looked up at Wilson and shook her head. "He asked me to marry him."

Wilson nodded and said nothing. He pulled out his phone and called Sue and asked her to come over as soon as she could.

Dot sat down in her wheelchair and stared at Brian lying there in that bed, almost dead.

He was the smartest man she had ever known. Why had he waited until this moment to ask her to marry him?

What in the world was he up to?

Chapter Twenty-nine

April 24th, 2022
Actual Earth Time
Location: Chicago

SHE SAT WITH Brian for another half hour, then decided she couldn't take it anymore. She had to do something and do it now.

Time really was running out.

Sue had gotten there a few minutes before and looking very worried. At one point Wilson had tucked the blankets around his father and told him to hang on.

Sue had taken out a stethoscope and listened to Brian's heart, then shook her head. "Not much longer."

There didn't seem to be anything they could do, or any doctor here on Earth could do. Brian's old body was just taking his final breaths.

Dot just couldn't let Brian die.

Not like this.

Not after all the times he had saved Earth.

This wasn't right or fair.

"I'll be right back," she said to Wilson and Sue.

Then taking her wheelchair, she walked behind it, pushing it ahead of her out of Brian's room and down the hall toward the nurse's station. Brian's meaning was clear as far as she was concerned. He wanted her to marry him and live in space. If she had anything to say about it, that was what she planned on doing.

She was going to get him out of here and back to his young body somehow.

She didn't know how, but she wasn't going to let him die without trying something.

It was the least the EPL could do. She just needed to point that out to a few generals, maybe at the top of her lungs.

The clock above the wall behind the nurse's station said it was only a few minutes after eleven in the morning.

The nurse on duty was a woman by the name of Joyce. She sometimes worked days, other times she worked nights. Joyce was often the one on duty when they went on missions. That was enough.

Joyce had a large smile, graying dark hair that was pulled back and tied, and bright green eyes. She looked middle-aged and wore a bright gold wedding ring. Joyce had always been nice and kind to Dot, something Dot appreciated.

Dot waited a moment until there was no one else within listening range, then leaned on the counter and said clearly to Joyce.

"Brian isn't going to make it through the day. I want to talk to one of the generals with the *EPL* and I won't take no for an answer."

Joyce looked stunned for a moment. Actually, more than stunned. Shocked.

Dot expected her to ask what exactly Dot was talking about, but instead Joyce looked in both directions to make sure no one was listening.

"General Brooks is aware of the situation with Captain Saber."

"Then tell him to get his ass on the phone to me in ten minutes," Dot said, her old voice taking on her captain traits and power. "I'll be in my room."

"Yes, Captain," Joyce said, nodding, a look of worry crossing her face.

That was the first time in four years anyone at Shady Valley Nursing Home had referred to her by her *League* rank.

"Tell the general to make it snappy," Dot said and turned, pushing her wheelchair ahead of her back down the hall toward her room, doing her best to keep her back straight and her walk steady.

The greatest captain in the long history of the *Earth Protection League* wasn't going to die today if she had anything to say about it.

And she planned on having a lot to say.

Chapter Thirty

April 24th, 2022
Actual Earth Time
Location: Chicago

BY THE TIME she got to her room, she had something figured out. Brian had asked her to marry him because he knew that was important in getting them off the planet.

It was the only reason for his timing like that. He knew something she didn't.

It wasn't a dying wish or a hope of a man wanting to not die.

Brian knew he was dying, and he knew that if they weren't getting married, the regulations wouldn't allow him to leave. Or some such stupid organizational rule like that.

That had to be the reason.

Dot made it to her room, pushed the door closed, and had just sat in her chair when her desk phone rang. It sounded odd to her ears, it seldom rang since her son wasn't much of a caller.

She took a deep breath and picked up the phone. Then, without so much as a hello, she said, "You have many bases out near the borders where humans from here are living and working and raising families. Correct?"

"That is correct," General Brooks said, his voice clearly hesitant.

"Including Steven's Base," she said, remembering where she and Brian had danced and spent two wonderful days just last week after saving Earth from a large moon.

"Yes," General Brooks said.

"Captain Saber's conditioned has worsened this morning," Dot said.

"We are aware of the captain's condition," General Brooks said.

"Are you aware," Dot said, making her voice very firm, "that Captain Saber asked me to marry him and I said yes."

There was a silence on the other end of the line. It was as if they had been disconnected, but it was clear they had not.

Dot waited for a moment, then went on, deciding to push the point.

"We want to start a family and keep working for the *League*," she said firmly. "I am assuming that is a condition to immigrating to that area of space."

She was taking a chance at that, because she didn't know for sure, but it again would make sense considering Brian's proposal of marriage. It hadn't been romantic, but it had given her some great ammunition to use to save his life.

"It is," General Brooks said after a moment. "Intent to start a family is required to settle in that area of space permanently."

Dot shook her head. Why hadn't she and Brian talked about this more, got this done long before now? Both of them were just so damned old-fashioned for their own good at times.

"We're planning on have a brood," she said, even though they had never really talked about having children. "A whole mess of little Sabers running around messing things up. Now get us the hell out of here before my future husband dies."

Again there was silence on the other end for a moment.

Then General Brooks said, "It's not that simple."

Dot barely kept herself from yelling. "Neither was saving this stupid planet a dozen times, including from that moon last week and all those Dog Warships three days ago. But Captain Saber and I have done just that for you. So with respect, General, I don't give a damn about simple. Get my future husband out of her. Alive. And do it quickly."

"Think this through," Captain," General Brooks said. "You will lose your family."

"You know my son lives on the West Coast and you know we are not close? Correct?" she asked.

"I know of your family," General Brooks said.

"I have said goodbye to my family a number of times over the years," Dot said. "Captain Saber is my family now. And I sure as hell don't want to lose him."

"I understand," General Brooks said.

"So get Captain Saber out of here now, give me a couple days to wrap up things here before I join him."

There was silence on the other end, so Dot kept pushing.

"Captain Saber and I are good breeding stock for your colony, wouldn't you say?"

"You're sure about this?" General Brooks asked one more time.

"I'm sure," she said. "But if you don't hurry, the option will be gone. He may go at any moment."

"That bad?" the General asked, clearly finally starting to understand what Dot had been saying all along. There was actual worry in that question.

"That bad," Dot said. "Why do you think I demanded this call now?"

Again there was silence for a moment.

"Thirty minutes," General Brooks said. "Work with the nurse to keep people away from his room. Get his sliding glass door open."

"How long will it take?" she asked.

"Five minutes to switch him out," General Brooks said.

"Done," Dot said.

And the line went dead.

Dot hung up the phone and took a deep breath before standing and heading for the door to her room and the nurse's station, pushing her wheelchair as quickly as she could in front of her.

Now if Brian could just hang on long enough to be rescued from old age.

Chapter Thirty-one

April 24th, 2022
Actual Earth Time
Location: Chicago

AS DOT APPROACHED the nurse's station, Joyce hung up the phone and nodded at her.

Dot suddenly felt like she was a spy in a cold war movie.

"I'll go in and get his door unlocked," Dot said. "His son and granddaughter are in there as well, so I'll ask to talk with them in the hall."

Joyce started to say something, but her phone rang.

Dot watched as Joyce listened for a moment, then hung up.

"They will be coming through Captain Saber's door in exactly ten minutes."

Dot glanced at the big clock on the wall. It was exactly twenty-one minutes after eleven. She turned back for Brian's room.

Joyce took a moment before she could get out from behind the nurse's station, so Dot almost beat her to Brian's room. Joyce held Brian's door open for her.

Inside the room, it took a moment for Dot's eyes to adjust to the dimness as the hallway door swung closed. Under the sheet and light blanket, she could see Brian was still breathing.

Oh, thank heavens. He still had a chance.

Joyce went right to him and checked his heartbeat quickly, then looked under one eyelid.

She shook her head. Dot wasn't sure what that meant, but it clearly wasn't good.

Sue stepped up beside Joyce. "Not long?"

"Very close," Joyce said. "They are coming."

"Goodbye, Grandpa," Sue said, leaning over and kissing her grandfather on the cheek.

Dot headed for the sliding door into the center court to unlatch it, but Wilson stood and said simply, "I'll get it, Captain."

He unlocked the sliding door, but didn't open it.

Then he turned and saluted Dot.

"I suppose it's time I introduce myself to my future step-mother. Commander Wilson Saber at your service, Captain. I assume dad never said anything about his entire family being involved in the *EPL*."

Dot stood there, her mouth open, not sure what to say.

She looked at Sue, then back at Wilson. Both Brian's son and grand-daughter were part of the *League*. Why hadn't Brian said something about that to her.

"Typical of him," Wilson said, shaking his head.

"Thank heavens you convinced them into doing a daylight extraction," Sue said to Dot. "I don't think he would have made it to later tonight as planned."

"I'm sure he wouldn't have," Joyce said.

"Yes, thank-you, Captain," Wilson said. "For saving my father's life."

"Joyce and I'll be outside guarding the door," Sue said, patting Dot's shoulder as she went past. "Thank you for saving my grandfather. And keep him alive until I can get out there, would you?"

There wasn't a thing Dot could say, so all she did was nod. She was too shocked at the moment to say anything.

And relieved that they were coming for Brian.

As the door to the hallway closed, the exterior door slid open and two men carrying a stretcher came in, followed by two others carrying another stretcher with a body on it.

One of the first men saluted Dot and Wilson, then went to the bed and quickly checked Brian.

"We got to move now," he said after a moment, his voice urgent, but in control.

The two quickly got Brian on the stretcher and as they did, Brian opened his eyes.

"Hang in there, dad," Wilson said. "I'll catch up with you in twenty years or so along the way."

Brian smiled.

"Try not to get yourself killed before I get out there," Wilson said.

"I don't think Captain Leeds is going to let that happen," Brian whispered, just loud enough for her and Wilson to hear.

Dot almost broke into tears right there. Just hearing him talk again was wonderful.

Then Brian closed his eyes and the two men rushed him out the door, vanishing as soon as they cleared the edge of the room.

The other two men quickly placed the other body on the bed. It looked exactly like Brian, right down to the old nightshirt stained with food. But this body was very, very dead.

They both nodded to Dot and Wilson and then stepped outside, vanishing almost instantly as they cleared the door.

Wilson went over and pulled the sliding glass door closed and made sure the drapes were in place to keep the room dim.

Dot stared at the dead husk on the bed. It looked like the old Brian, but she knew it wasn't.

Then she turned to Wilson who was also staring at the body under the sheet on the bed. "You and the *League* had no intention of letting him die, did you?"

Wilson shook his head. "They were going to make an exception to the marriage policy for him. But it seems they didn't need to."

"You planned on taking him out tonight?"

Wilson nodded. "I don't think he would have made it. Thank you again for pushing the general and saving Dad's life."

"Let's hope he survived," Dot said. "From my understanding, it sometimes takes time to get those transport ships going."

"They'll save him," Wilson said. "They'll just put him on a warship and jump him a few years if it's coming down to that, before putting him on a transport."

She nodded. "Of course."

"Just wish I could make the wedding," Wilson said. "But someone would have to change my diapers if I tried it."

"We'll send you pictures," Dot said, laughing for the first time in days and days. And that felt wonderful.

More wonderful than she wanted to admit right now.

Wilson smiled back, then looked at the body on the bed. "Guess I have some phone calls to make and a funeral to attend. Makes it a lot easier knowing he's going to be out there alive, and with you."

Dot touched Wilson's arm and then pushed her chair out of the room as Wilson held the door for her.

Joyce and Sue were standing in the hallway watching them come out.

"They got him away," Wilson said.

Both Joyce and Sue nodded.

At that moment, Sue's cell phone rang.

She looked annoyed, but glanced at it and then answered it.

After a long moment of listening, she said simply, "Thank you, General. I'll pass the word."

She looked at the other three. "He made it, but barely. They jumped him a few years away to make sure and then put him on a larger transport to Davis Station."

Dot felt her knees get weak, but Wilson slipped a hand under her arm and steadied her as she held the handles on her wheelchair.

Sue smiled at Dot. "The general had a message for you. He said to tell you that Captain Saber will be waiting for you on Steven's Base. It seems you have a wedding to plan and some dancing to do."

At that, Dot simply moved around her wheelchair and sat down.

One Last Trip Out
Four Nights Later

Chapter Thirty-two

April 28th, 2022
Actual Earth Time
Location: Chicago

IT SURPRISED DOT that she had so few "affairs" she had to wrap up. After living in assisted care for over twenty years, she didn't have much, and the insurance money from the settlement from the car accident, that had killed her first husband and crippled her, would go to her son in her will. She had spent very, very little of it over the years. That money would make his life easier, and she had put some of it in trusts for her grandchildren's college education.

There just hadn't been much for her to to spend money on considering she was crippled and her living in Shady Valley was paid for in the settlement.

The worst part of getting everything in order had come with the phone call to her son and two grandkids. She really couldn't say goodbye, but she sort of did anyway. She would miss them, even though she seldom saw them.

She hoped they would miss her, even though the grandkids didn't really know her at all. They had lived so far away for so long, and there had been so few visits.

Shady Valley Nursing Home had a small memorial service for Brian, but Dot had claimed she wasn't feeling well and had skipped it. She just didn't feel much like mourning the man she would be marrying very shortly.

That just seemed wrong in so many ways.

And she really didn't know anyone else who lived here, since she had spent all her time with Brian over the years, especially the last four.

It would have been another matter if he hadn't made it out in time.

A totally different matter, actually.

She didn't want to let herself think about that at all. He had made it and was young and waiting for her. That was all that mattered.

So finally, on the fourth morning after Brian left, when Lieutenant Sherri came to wake her up at a little after three in the morning, Dot was ready to go.

And she surprisingly had no regrets.

All she could see was a bright and happy future ahead.

"I hear congratulations are in order," Lieutenant Sherri said, smiling as she helped Dot out of her bed and made sure her wheelchair was there and sturdy to hold onto.

"I guess so," Dot said. "I understand I have a fiancé waiting for me at Steven's Base. Seems we have a wedding to plan."

"I hear it's beautiful there," the lieutenant said as they started for the doorway to the hallway, Dot holding onto the lieutenant's arm and walking slowly to let her old legs get going again.

In the hallway Joyce was standing there, smiling. "I'll miss you, Captain."

Dot indicated that Joyce should give her a hug.

The nurse did.

"Thank you for your help in saving Brian," Dot said, smiling at Joyce.

"You are more than welcome," Joyce said. "And I hope to be out your way in about thirty more years or so."

Dot laughed. "You'll be young and I'll be middle-aged by that point. Sometimes this is just very strange."

Joyce laughed.

"I'll be about twenty years behind her," Lieutenant Sherri said.

And all three of them laughed at how they would all be back in their same ages they were now by that point.

"Look us up," Dot said, marveling at the fact that when Lieutenant Sherri got out there, Dot and Brian would be old again and the lieutenant would look just as she did now. But fifty years will have passed.

With one last wave to Joyce, Dot and Lieutenant Sherri moved slowly into Brian's empty room. It had been cleaned and was waiting for the next resident.

Dot wondered if that resident would be a recruit for the *EPL*. More than likely, they would put one in her room and one in Brian's again since Joyce was already working here. It just made extraction easier.

Outside, in the center courtyard, the spring night air had a bite to it, but Dot didn't care. It was her last night on Earth.

She had loved Chicago. She had loved watching the seasons here through the windows over the last twenty-plus years.

But she wouldn't really miss it.

A moment later the yellow light from above took her and the lieutenant up into the transport ship.

Lieutenant Sherri helped her into the coffin-like sleep chamber one last time and stepped back and saluted.

"It has been an honor to serve you, Captain," she said.

"The honor has been mine to serve with you," Dot said. "See you in about fifty years."

"That's a promise I'll hold you to, Captain," Lieutenant Sherri said, then closed the lid to the sleep chamber.

She did her standard two taps to tell Dot it was secure.

And a moment later Dot was asleep.

Chapter Thirty-three

April 28th, 2022
Equivalent Earth Time
Location: Deep Space

ONCE AGAIN DOT awoke from the deep sleep and pushed the lid to her coffin open, reveling in the feeling of being young again.

After being in that old body, this just never got old.

Her skin was smooth, her hair full and brown and not brittle.

And her legs worked.

She levered herself out of the coffin and landed on her feet, enjoying the feeling of standing on them without worrying about falling. And without the aches that came with trying to walk.

She stripped off her old-lady nightgown and tossed it back into the coffin. She wouldn't need it again. But she would let someone else throw it away.

Back on Earth, her son would be getting a phone call that she had passed away easily in her sleep. He would be upset, but her leaving would make life easier on him and his children. There was a lot more money in her estate than he knew about, and that would surprise him.

She just wished she could see his face when he discovered that.

She would miss him and her grandchildren, she had no doubt. But she would survive.

And so would they. That was the nature of death.

But she wasn't dead. She was getting a chance to be reborn in a brand new home, and that had her excited.

She got her uniform out of the closet and got dressed, enjoying the feel of the

silk blouse and the photon stunner on her hip.

She looked to be in her mid-twenties this time and she assumed she was at Steven's Base. But she wasn't sure. This was clearly her cabin on *The Blooming Rose*. So no telling exactly where she was.

But now she got to stay in this young body, not go back to the old, crippled body.

This was the body she remembered.

Finally ready, she opened her door and stepped into the hallway.

There were people on both sides of her door.

Everyone snapped to attention and saluted.

She laughed at first, smiling and looking for Brian. This had to be his doing, but she didn't see him.

She saluted back and then everyone broke into cheers, welcoming her.

Marian Knudson from Brian's ship stood next to Steve and both Dot's crew and Brian's crew were mingled and cheering and shouting welcome and congratulations on the coming marriage to her.

Then from down the hall she heard a loud "Attention!"

Everyone stopped and again snapped to attention, holding their salutes.

Through them came the most handsome man she had ever seen, making an entrance from an old Hollywood movie.

Once again the sight of him just took her breath away.

Captain Brian Saber stopped in front of her and keeping a strictly military face, also saluted.

All she wanted to do was shout and jump on him, but somehow she managed to hold herself together, staring at the man she loved more than she could ever imagine loving anyone.

Finally, letting him hold his salute just an extra second or so, she saluted back.

Brian snapped off his salute and said with a smile on his face to everyone in the hallway, "As you were."

Everyone went back to cheering as he said simply to her through the noise, "I love you."

Then she kissed him and felt him kiss her back and felt his wonderful, strong arms around her.

And she knew she was home.

~

Now Available
from all your favorite booksellers
in trade paper and electronic editions.

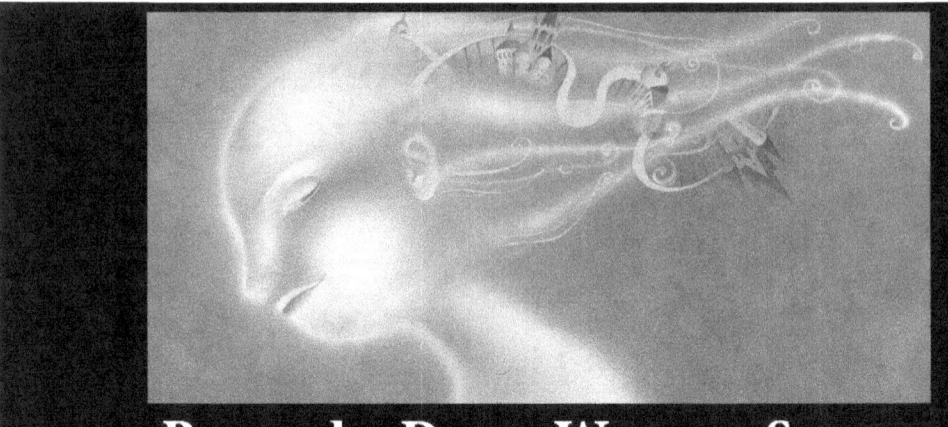

Poems by DEAN WESLEY SMITH

Button

Lightly, I flick its button
to turn it on, laughing.

My cash register reminds me
of a girl I once knew.

She had a button,
and she took my money, too.

Cold Buttered Feelings

In most states, two movie tickets,
a box of popcorn,
and a coke
cost $2.67 more
than a marriage license.